CIRCLES IN THE SPIRAL

a novel

Shane Joseph

Circles in the Spiral
Copyright © 2020 Shane Joseph
All rights reserved
Published by Blue Denim Press Inc.
First Edition
ISBN 978-1-927882-52-8

This is a work of fiction. Resemblances to persons living or dead, or to
organizations, are unintended and purely co-incidental.

Cover Design by Shane Joseph.
Cover photography by Ken Solilo
Typeset in Windlass, Cambria and Garamond

Library and Archives Canada Cataloguing in Publication

Title: Circles in the spiral / Shane Joseph.
Names: Joseph, Shane, 1955- author.
Identifiers: Canadiana (print) 2020027399X | Canadiana (ebook)
20200274015 | ISBN 9781927882528
   (softcover) | ISBN 9781927882535 (Kindle) | ISBN
9781927882542 (EPUB)
Classification: LCC PS8619.O846 C57 2020 | DDC C813/.6—
dc23

"Progress has not followed a straight ascending line, but a spiral with rhythms of progress and retrogression, of evolution and dissolution."

~ Johann Wolfgang von Goethe

Chapter 1

I flung the squeeze ball at the wall and watched it rebound onto the floor, bounce once, and roll under the sofa like the story of my life. Damn, this plot wasn't working. It was more of the same.

"Give me something fresh," my agent, Sam, had said. "Sales are flagging."

So was my life.

All fiction is contrivance—didn't Sam get it? It's about tossing a bunch of possibilities in the air and threading them through to a satisfactory conclusion before they hit the floor. But after awhile, like a sleepwalker, we trace our steps over familiar routes because they are comfortable footpaths. Did I know what went through the viscount's mind when he removed the lady's garter? We know *what* is around the next corner, we know *when* a new twist is overdue, and we know *how* to tie all those loose ends we planted deliberately, but we don't know *why*. We lack depth when the age we are depicting is not our own and when we project our own sensibilities on another time. It wasn't working anymore; my agent was right. And in the meantime, younger writers were inventing newer forms: mythopoeia, cli-fi, bizarro, interactive, fan-fic, gran-lit, auto-fic. My traditional historical adventure story was dated. I had no answer. All I had were bad dreams, but that's for later.

"Write about your own life," Susan had urged me one day when I was stuck in one of these doomsday spirals. She had been reading too much Knausgaard.

"My achieve-nothing life?" I countered. "What's so exciting about that? Nah."

Now, I went looking for my squeezie. My back arched as I grabbed the fuzzy ball from under the sofa where it had rolled, next to an old baseball cap that had gone missing weeks ago. I felt a crick and a stab of pain. I couldn't rise—darn, the damned back had gone again! I squeezed the ball to transfer my pain to it and rolled over into a supine position. From there I surveyed the cobwebs on the ceiling I should have cleaned out weeks ago as the pain travelled down my back and into my legs. Too much stacking of produce at the grocery store, my part time job, that was the reason for the back to go; recently I had been working more shifts to cover my cash flow requirements.

I must have lain there for an hour before the pain eased sufficiently to allow me to limp back to my desk. Pulling myself into the chair, I stared at my unfinished novel: five chapters in and twenty-five more to go, if I were to follow my tried and true recipe. But this time I knew I was never going to finish this sucker. I did not *want* to finish this sucker. I was sick of the formula; readers were sick of the formula. Working the night shift at the factory and the day shift at the grocery store loomed as the only ways to feed myself and pay the bills, since Susan had departed with the accountant.

I thought fondly of Susan. Thirty-five and ten years younger than me, with her biological clock ticking down to zero hour and unable to have a child with me because we couldn't afford one. It was always that next novel that was going to be our ticket to raising a family, but six novels later no ground had been broken, no ground had moved, either—for both of us. There were other reasons for not having children, but I wasn't letting Susan into that side of the closet. The young accountant had been a surer bet for her. Besides, he had a steadier and larger paycheque, and she could take time off from her teaching job to raise a family. No, I wasn't bitter.

What was I saying? You bet I was fucking bitter!

As for the bad dreams, they had been a part of my life for as long as I could remember. I wondered whether I would have a nervous breakdown if they suddenly went away. Withdrawal symptoms of the next kind. I had found fiction writing to be a panacea for the dreams because I couldn't afford a shrink. And it had helped, particularly when my writing was on the up and up. All those demons who plagued me during sleep got turned into characters in my books and that seemed to please the goblins, for a while at least. But now that I was blocked and fading on the popularity meter, those dreams—nay, nightmares—were making a return with a vengeance.

I had been googling, not writing, while ruminating on the past and wondering about my future. I popped into my email to see if there was any fan mail. Fan mail was always invigorating for it made this lonely profession worthwhile. There was none today. However, besides the various solicitations for penis enlargements, Viagra, and costume jewellery, there was an e-mail promoting wellness. At first glance, it appeared to be one of those personalized ones that are mass mailed by marketing websites to clients' mailing lists—first 1000 contacts free—and after we have hooked up your entire business to our platform, it will cost dollars and dollars for subsequent mailings, dear sucker! But this one looked like it was speaking to me at this particular point of my life; it had the background of an Ontario lakeside scene and was calming and alluring. I clicked on the link provided for more information.

A website popped up on my screen. This website was weird. It only had the sketched face of a bearded man with twinkling eyes and a flashing question: *Stuck in a rut?*

You bet I was! The man's gaze was hypnotic and seemed to be beckoning me. I clicked on his face, which was a giant hyperlink, and it took me to photographs of a row of cabins beside a lake, somewhere in rural Ontario with lush hills in the background. *Find your inner voice in a serene setting*, it began. . .

As I read, I figured this was probably what I needed. To get away from my present reality and recharge. I still had enough money in my overdraft to pay for three days instead of the customary week's stay expected at this refuge, located about three hours north on the shores of a lake whose indigenous name I couldn't even pronounce. As for paying the overdraft, I'd worry about that when I got back. *Live in the moment,* was one of the platitudes in the retreat's description, and even if it was most probably a lot of New Age bullshit, I would have a lake, a cabin, and some privacy. A change of scene in which my plot could be redrawn. All in three days.

I signed up online.

A week later, the old Honda made it through the three-hour drive to the resort. I passed a lot of cottages beside tiny lakes where urban dwellers had originally fled to escape the rat race but had now found their shacks turning into real estate boomtowns. Today, those former shacks sat beside two-storey, Shack 2.0 structures packed with every modern convenience. I wondered why the city slickers kept those old shacks hanging around—memento mori or benchmarks to remind them how far they had ascended the social and wealth scales?

When I drove up to the line of cabins by the lake, they looked as described in the website, not like those fake B&Bs shot with fisheye lenses and posted online to trap consumers. Between the cabins, and through a ring of tall poplars, the lake peeped through. The temperature was suddenly cool on this humid summer afternoon.

Where was the office? Didn't I have to check in or something? All seven cabins looked alike in size and colour. I tried the one directly facing the parking lot, the middle one. I had guessed right. The inner room— and there was only one large room—was devoid of furniture except for a desk and chair, and a large mat in the centre with a bundle of blankets upon it. A deep "mmmm" emanated from somewhere. I suddenly realized it was coming from the bundle that had started to move. A bald human head emerged, similar to the caricature I had seen on the website. A pair of eyes blinked open and that twinkle re-appeared—it was the real deal.

"Ah, you are William. William Smallwood. Welcome."

"Call me Will. Guru Swaminanda?"

The guru emerged from the pile of blankets, and he was stark naked. His belly was flat, and his ribs protruded, but his penis dangled a good ten inches over well hung balls.

"Sorry, I caught you at a private moment."

"There is no privacy here. We are constantly in the moment." The guru pulled out a well-thumbed register from a drawer in the desk and opened to a page. "I have to follow the legal requirements and ask you to write your name and address. Afterwards, you are free to do what inspires you here." He had a slight accent, but he seemed like he had lived in the west for a long time.

As I wrote my details in the book, I noticed there were four other guests who had checked in for the week, four days earlier: a couple by the surname of Davis from Toronto, a man who described himself as Professor Darlington PhD, and a woman called Divine Secrets from the Ottawa area, my beat—I wondered what her profession was with a name like that.

The guru hadn't bothered to put on any clothes while I was thus occupied. He scratched his crotch absent mindedly and said, "We eat in the communal hall, it's a cabana by the lake directly downhill from here, at seven p.m. every day. Breakfast is at seven a.m. in the same cabana, and no food is served during the day for that is when we empty the body and fill the mind. Your cabin is number six at the eastern edge. I will see you at seven p.m. for dinner, and I will introduce you to everyone else, if you don't bump into them in the meantime."

"You had advertised meditation sessions. I'd like to take some."

"Yes, I do them at ten a.m. and at nine p.m. for my guests. I also have one-on-one counselling sessions for those that need it. From the online form you filled out, I would say you need it." His eyes peered closely at me, trapping me in his gaze.

By the time I got to my cabin, I had signed up for a meditation session at ten a.m. and a counselling session at four p.m. the following day. That was enough to assuage myself that I had done the minimum, the rest was up to me.

My cabin was similarly furnished to the guru's. I plugged in my laptop and pulled the desk over to the window overlooking the lake. The water was still—no powerboats on this lake, thank God—like a blue pool cover thrown over from shore to shore. It was cool inside the cabin. I spotted a Muskoka chair on a pier to my left, away from the cottages. A very large man sat in it wearing only a panama hat and a heavy gold chain, smoking a cigar. His body glistened with lotion and was a toasty red. He was wielding a pair of binoculars, checking out the birds swirling over the lake. Occasionally he swung the instrument towards the shore, towards the other end of the line of cottages. I followed the angle of his sight and spotted a woman sitting under a giant spruce close to the bank of the lake; she seemed to be sketching in a pad on her lap. She wore a loose dress, relieving me of the fear that I had arrived at a nudist colony. She would look up occasionally from her work, gaze off towards the distant shore, then return to the pad. I surmised that I had just met Professor Darlington trying to divine the secrets of the artist by the same name.

To confirm my assumption, loud noises erupted from the cabin adjacent to me, #7. I slid open the door leading to the small deck of my cabin, and the voices increased in volume. A man and a woman were on the deck next door, arguing.

"They want money again. What the fuck is wrong?" the man was saying. He had a deep voice, and I imagined him to be overweight.

"University is expensive. Two kids cost." The woman's voice was high pitched, tense. An angular woman? A perverse thought of the two of them in bed, him on top, flashed through my mind.

"It was your idea to have them so close together."

"If you know what it is to change diapers and smell shitty backsides, you'd not have had them at all."

"You wanted to get back to work. That's why?"

Were they arguing about decisions they'd made, perhaps, twenty years ago? I edged closer to the screen door to hear better.

"So, what are you going to do?" the woman was saying. "We can't be enjoying ourselves here while our poor kids are starving?"

"You call this enjoying? We starve during the day and there isn't even a glass of wine at dinner."

"You're not deprived. There are so many empties in our cabin, you'll have to make another run to the LCBO soon."

There was a creaking and cracking as if a heavy weight had settled into one of the deck chairs. "I guess I'll just wire Josh the money to shut him up. But that's it."

"You can't leave Meghan out."

"Oh yes, they chose universities across the country, yet they know what we ate for breakfast."

"Social media, honey. And catch-up summer classes will do that for them."

"If they were smart, they wouldn't need to catch up. They'd be working summer jobs."

"We can't let them drop out. Not now."

"Too many frat parties is what I think is happening."

"We had our parties too."

"Hmmph."

There was a clicking of computer keys of some sort. Then, "Okay, wired, done. Both. I don't want to hear from them until Thanksgiving."

"Another glass of wine, honey?" The woman's voice had softened, but only a tad.

I shut the door. I had just met the Davises.

I went for a walk before dinner. The property ran up wooded hills north of the lake, and the water was visible through the assorted pine, birch and maple trees whenever I stopped to catch my breath. The maples were just starting to turn colour, but at least a month of warm weather lay ahead of us. I circled the property, headed downhill and veered left to my cottage along a pathway that ran parallel to the shore. The dining room cabana, south of the middle cottage, erected on piles over the water and accessible only by a narrow pier, was open on all sides with only supporting beams for walls; a dark-featured cook was busy over an open cooking range at the shore end, and the smells of simmering food tinged with oriental spices were inviting. As I neared the spot where the woman had been sketching, I saw her rising and dusting the leaves off her ankle-length, pastel dress with faded floral motifs. I didn't think she was wearing any underclothes, and when she raised her arms to arrange the straw hat on her head there were lush growths of hair under her arms. She had an intelligent face with light eyes and a well-proportioned body. About thirty-five, I estimated, and a hippy throwback or a contemporary woman sick of lotions and depilatories. I had not kept pace with contemporary body fashions during my pre-occupation with sterile historical fiction, so I couldn't tell which was which.

"Hi," I said, stepping off the path and moving towards her. "I've just arrived. I'm Will."

She had a radiant smile although her features were somewhat drawn. "My spiritual name is Divine. My family calls me Dee."

"I like Dee. Did the lake inspire you today?"

"It always inspires me. I grew up on one. Then I had to move to the city."

I fell in step with her and noticed that we were walking in the direction of my cottage.

"I'm a writer. But I've lost my groove." It felt odd unburdening like this, and my words came in a rush. But I felt I could do it with this woman. It was easier with unknown persons whom I would never meet again after I returned to my city nook.

"It happened to me too. I was doing commercial paintings for corporations. I was good at it and made a lot of money. But I wasn't creating what I wanted, just throwing in things that positioned my patrons well. I had a complete breakdown three years ago. Guru Swaminanda cured me." That accounted for her strained features. Faces take the longest to recover from the ravages of ill fortune. Faces don't tell lies.

"Then there is hope for me," I said.

"You have to be prepared to let go. Many of us aren't."

An image of the Davises flashed before me. Were they ready to let go? Was the peeping tom, Professor Darlington—if that were indeed him—ready? Was I?

"You have a leg up on the rest of us here," I said, as the ensemble of guests flowed through my mind.

"Professor Darlington, if you haven't met him yet you will at dinner, is the furthest from finding his way. He is in cottage number four."

"I watched him observing you through his binoculars."

She laughed gently. "I indulge him. That seems to be the only way I can help him. Ogling and lusting assuages his ego better than words, for he never listens."

My palms were getting clammy with her directness.

We had reached cottage number five, the other one next to mine.

"I need to go in and meditate before dinner," Dee said. She faced me and flashed a sad smile. "When you are ready, and if you need my help, let me know." Her eyes were inviting. Then she turned on her heel and went up the path to her door, leaving me to stare at her curvy bottom swaying under the flimsy pastel dress, wondering whether her offer of help would extend to sex.

She paused at the doorway and turned around. "I might need your help too," she said quickly before heading inside.

"I prefer Schopenhauer's views on sex." Professor Darlington pushed back his chair, tilting it at a forty-five-degree angle and tapping fingers on his stomach, distended by the excellent meal we had just partaken of chapatis, dhal, aloo ghobi, chana masala and raita, all washed down with copious quantities of lassi. He eyed Dee sitting across from him as he spoke, and she ignored him. Darlington had graced us by covering his earlier nakedness with a pair of khaki shorts and a resort cotton shirt, the three top buttons undone to reveal his metal chain. He had a broad forehead and trimmed gray beard that accentuated his professorial air, and he smiled to himself every time he delivered one of his declarative statements, as if silently challenging anyone to match his erudition.

We were sitting around the circular table in the centre of the cabana. Dinner had lasted over an hour even though the meal was buffet style. Darlington had been pontificating philosophy, particularly on the subject of reproductive rights, the male sexual drive, and colonial influences on art, all aimed at Dee while she had been calmly deflecting his thrusts. The Davises, dressed like they were going to an elegant city party, replete with a tie for him and earrings for her, had looked inebriated when they arrived at the cabana and had difficulty following the discussion. After asking a question or two and getting circulatory answers from Darlington, they slumped back into their food—eager to finish and return to their private wine stash. Guru Swaminanda, dressed in a flowing white kaftan, had been quiet during the meal; like me, he had been the observer. But I noticed one difference: while Darlington looked upon Dee with haughtiness and a determination to dominate, the guru looked upon her with deep admiration, even love. Occasionally he looked across at Darlington warily.

"Schopenhauer was a misogynist," Dee suddenly burst out. "He cloaked himself in Buddhism, just like philosophers…and teachers…" here she paused to look directly at the professor, then turned her head towards the guru, "…like to cloak themselves in intriguing philosophy to convey their mystique. But deep down he was a dirty old man, a woman beater, and a pederast." A dam, that had been well reinforced throughout the meal, seemed to have finally burst. Her cheeks flamed red, which matched the fresh dress she had changed into; and she was wearing a black bra underneath, I could see, from the straps that edged out at her shoulder.

The guru cleared his throat at this point and raised his hand as if to quell further verbal sparring between his guests. "I think we need to understand why we are here. We are all on a journey of self discovery and self mastery. The answers we are looking for lie within us, not in the teachings of other mortals with their own problems."

Davis burped and laughed. "You mean to say that I'm paying for my kids to go to university to study a pile of bullshit? Hey, Marge, got that?" He turned and shook his wife by the shoulder. She dusted his hand off and looked out across the twilit lake.

Darlington came back, right on cue. "Your money is not wasted, Phil. For one, it pays my salary. We are there to distil knowledge that grows exponentially each year into digestible forms for our students."

"Gatekeepers of knowledge have a greater responsibility towards their charges," the guru said.

"I was simply trying to make the point that sex is a life force, and we should not fear it or shun it, in all its forms," Darlington said, the self-satisfied, half grin re-emerging. *Top that*, it suggested.

I decided to add my contribution. "Then it would be better to get out there and have a good fuck rather than imagine it through the lenses of a pair of binoculars."

I felt Dee's warm hand grip my arm in gratitude as the professor abruptly let go his tilting chair to lean forward but ended up going over backwards, crashing on the floor, his feet kicking over our table and scattering us in disarray. I hadn't realized my words would be so powerful. If I could only write that way!

The professor painfully picked himself up from the floor and straightened his chair as the rest of the guests tried to get out of the detritus he had strewn. Darlington didn't look too rosy standing upright, for one side of his body now looked out of sync with the other. A slipped lumbar joint? Ouch, that would hurt for the next little while! The cook hurried over with a wet cloth to mop up the curries and other food spilt on the floor. Mrs. Davis was trying to wipe a splash of brown from her eggshell dinner dress. I noticed the guru had remained in his seat, the only person unmoved in the fracas; his eyes were closed.

"You should talk, Mr. Writer," the professor grimaced. I regretted having told the gathering what I did for a living during introductions when we had first gathered for dinner. "You have sex on the pages of your books. I don't see anything *real* in that."

I bit my tongue. The professor was right.

"Philip, it's late. We should leave." Mrs. Davis had given up trying to wipe the damage off her dress and dumped her soiled napkin on the now straightened table. She grabbed her husband's hand firmly and yanked his bulk into standing position. "We will see you all in the morning. And hopefully, tomorrow we can talk about more pleasant subjects, like birds. Good night." They staggered down the flame-lit pathway to their cabin.

The guru spoke again with his eyes still closed. "Tonight has revealed that we still have a lot of work to do on ourselves."

As we were leaving the cabana, the guru held Dee's hands in his and bade her a good night. He looked sad to see her depart.

I walked Dee back to her cabin for fear that Darlington might try to inflict his revenge on her, for his cabin was next door. "Lock your door tonight," I advised Dee as we made our way down the pathway with its jagged flashes of torchlight.

"I lock it every night. Professor 'Darling' got particularly pissed off after he walked over to my cabin the first night we arrived and asked whether we could gaze into each other's navels, literally. And I refused him."

I laughed. "He said that?"

She laughed too. Then we quieted as we were passing the professor's cabin where the light was on inside, for he had left—or should I say, limped from—the cabana ahead of us.

At her door, she paused. "I would invite you in to act as my bodyguard through the night." Her look was sincere, open. She had mastered the art of letting go, of honesty, while the rest of us, perhaps apart from the guru, were still trapped in our assumed roles.

"You mean, to sleep with you?" I was surprised at my boldness, perhaps I was trying to practice letting go too, but my armpits were clammy. Damn it, but I so wanted her to say "yes."

"Yes. But now is not the right time."

I was crushed. I felt exactly how Professor Darlington must have felt on his first night at this place.

Off to the side, I thought I saw a curtain flutter in the illuminated cabin next door, and as I turned for a clearer view, Dee gave me a quick peck on my exposed cheek. My whole face tingled as if hit by a current, and I remained rooted to the spot, wanting the feeling to last forever. When was the last time I had been kissed, and with feeling? Eons ago, when Susan and I had been passionate for each other, before our ice age arrived and fractured us apart. I turned and reached forward to kiss Dee back, but she was already inside her door, shutting it silently behind her, leaving a quiet, "Sleep well," floating in the air.

I was floating somewhere, a black dot in a sea of white drawing me into another dimension. I was scared to cross over at first but then I yielded. It was like being in one of those low flying aircraft that went over mountain edges and yet you knew you were safe from plunging into the depths. A hum echoed in my ears, an "ommm," and I realized it was coming from within me. This floating was ethereal, I didn't care about the book anymore, or bills, or all the missed opportunities in my life. Was I dead?

I didn't know how long it lasted, but I was totally relaxed and didn't want the moment to end. But it was ending. The dot was spinning away from me, becoming smaller and smaller, and outside—birds chirping, an engine starting up somewhere, a dog barking—the world was returning to claim me. I opened my eyes.

The guru was in lotus position opposite me. The walls of his cabin surrounded us.

"How long have I been…out?" I asked, blinking.

"Does it matter?"

"I guess not. I wanted it to last longer. It was far better than my usual nightmares."

"You can do it any time you want, now that you know how."

"Beats smoking a joint."

"What insights did you receive?"

"I can't remember. I was just enjoying the ride."

The guru smiled. "Okay, I will forgive you this first time. But as you practice, you will start to receive and remember the messages you receive. Act on them when you are awake, and life will become more integrated."

There was a tap at the door. The guru looked towards it longingly. "My next appointment."

I rose unsteadily and rolled up my mat. "I guess I'll see you at four o'clock this afternoon for our counselling session." Suddenly, I was determined to let go all my burdens on him. The walls insulating my solitary existence were coming down.

When I opened the door, Dee stood on the step, a meditation mat rolled up under her arm. She was dressed in a sleeveless, batik-patterned dress and nothing else; she was barefoot. I exhaled slowly as I drank her in, waves of desire replacing the euphoria I had just experienced from the meditation.

She threw me a sunny smile. "Hope I didn't interrupt."

"No, I was just leaving." We were always passing each other in doorways, it seemed. I wanted to grab her and kiss her and put yesterday's unfinished business to bed, but the guru's presence held me off. I stammered something about seeing her later and slunk away.

I hiked up the hill and sat down in the shade of a maple, having a clear view of the lake. A canoe was struggling to get waterborne just off the pier, and in it I recognised the life-vested pair of Phil and Marge Davis. They were arguing about which way to paddle and as a result were stuck in the same place. Eventually, they seemed to get the hang of it and headed into the middle of the lake.

Leaves crackled behind me, and I saw the professor advance through the thicker undergrowth. He was wearing only beach shorts, the ubiquitous binoculars hanging from his neck competed with the gold chain for dominance. He saw me and began to walk away downhill. The meditation had left me in a placid mood, and I called after him.

"I'm sorry. I was out of turn last night."

He stopped in his tracks. Perhaps I had given him the opening he was seeking for he turned around immediately, a wide grin on his face.

"Glad I made a point with you," he said, settling down on a rock about ten feet away that was close to a disused well with crumbling stonework around it. He applied the binoculars to his eyes and gazed out upon the lake. I walked up to the well and gazed down—it was deep and packed with muddy debris at the bottom. In its open state it was a hazard; I wondered how many animals, or even humans, had walked into its gaping maw on an overcast night.

As if anticipating my question, Darlington said, "This place needs fixing up."

I moved away from the well and sat on a piece of broken-off masonry.

Darlington was surveying the Davises. "Those two will drown," he declared. "They don't know squat about canoeing."

"Why did you come out here?" I asked.

His lips curled down as he smiled. "I am a regular here. This time, I want to debunk the theory of mysticism."

"While the rest of us are trying to find answers to life through it."

"Life is what you make of it. Mysticism, Politics, Religion—they are all cloaks we throw on ourselves to cop out from the real work ahead."

"And what is the real work?"

"Satisfying the senses. And procreation. And then you die."

"A hedonistic atheist. This is the wrong place for you."

"I get a lot of satisfaction here when I meet the right people. But I'm only here for the week this time. Sufficient to write my exposé on this snake oil industry. Just like I did on the Church and on the Conservative Party."

"Does the guru know that you are trying to undermine him?"

"He is a fraud, you know. He is sleeping with Divine Secrets."

A knife cut through me at his words. But then it all added up: the looks and gestures I had seen exchanged between the guru and Dee, her repeated tours of this place after the guru had "cured" her, her provocative dress when visiting the man in private. And they could be banging each other at this very moment while we sat here uselessly debating universal truths.

"Are you sure these are not the words of a jilted suitor?"

"You didn't fair too well yourself last night, did you?" He was looking at me like a man peering over reading glasses, except that he wasn't wearing any.

I rose and dusted leaves and sand off my pants. "Well, each to his own. I have to be off to do some writing."

"Would you put the two of them copulating in your book?" A deep chuckle emanated from him.

"I write historical fiction. Napoleonic to Victorian eras. Copulation is never described in great detail. Sorry to disappoint you." I walked downhill leaving him struggling for a comeback.

Needless to say, Darlington had shattered the last vestiges of peace I had found through my recent meditation. I wondered whether I could re-conjure it in the sanctity of my cabin without allowing the disturbing image of the guru wielding his ten-inch cock on a suppliant Dee to intrude.

I was unable to reconstruct the meditation back in my cabin. Every time I closed my eyes, weird, carnal images emerged. And then those goblins, my lifelong companions started interloping too. I gave up and pulled out my manuscript that I had toted along on this trip. I usually took a hard copy of a work-in-progress with me wherever I went and made scribbles on it as new ideas for refinements occurred. But there were no new ideas today. I looked at the pile of papers, sick to my stomach at what I had created. And talking about my stomach, it was growling for lack of a midday meal. I pulled out a toke from my bag, went out on the deck, and smoked it to calm down. Thankfully, my neighbours were not in their cabin, so my fumes didn't offend anyone. I could see the Davises on the small beach by the cabana sprawled in deck chairs, roasting in the sun.

When I went to meet with the guru for my counselling session at four o'clock, I was in a foul mood, the marijuana had only dented the deep chasm of despair I was hovering over and made me hungrier. He took one look at me and said, "You are troubled. Sit down and talk to me."

I looked around the bare room, surveying every corner for signs of rabid lovemaking, sniffing the air for its tell-tale scents, even for the smell of that dead giveaway, air freshener, ready to flee at the first hint of betrayal. None were in evidence. Either I was imagining the worst, or the guru was an expert at wiping out his sins. I sat down on the mat opposite him. The despair flooded over. Looking into his benign eyes that held no hint of accusation, unlike mine, I broke down. I began unburdening. I must have spoken uninterrupted for about an hour, retracing my unrealized life as a writer, and when I finished, I was weeping. I hadn't even gone into my sorry past *before* I became a writer—that part was just too painful to get into.

"You carry a lot within you," the guru said when I had slumped into an exhausted silence. "I'm told that writers write because they seek to unburden and create order out of their chaotic lives. Your writing has not helped you. It has added to your burden."

"I don't believe in what I am writing now. I sold out to a pulp machine called commercial publishing."

"What did you seek to achieve through it?"

"Fame. Recognition. Money."

"And did you achieve these things?"

"In varying degrees. But they vanish quickly and have to be constantly restocked with another book, and another, with diminishing returns each time. I barely have the energy to re-stock shelves in my day job. I don't have the energy or the desire to do it in this one anymore."

"Then you should give it up before it takes a further toll on your health."

"What will I replace it with? I will have to work *three* dead-end jobs to make do."

"Write about what matters to you. Even if it's for your eyes only. You will be writing to heal, not to harm. As for money, recognition, and all that, they will continue to be illusory no matter how famous you become."

"How do I give up something that has become second nature to me, even though I dislike it?"

"Like a cancer. You cut it, burn it, or poison it. The separation must be tangible and deliberate to be lasting." Then the guru's voice took on a reflective, regretful tone, and my ears pricked up. "We all have unhealthy attachments that hold us back, and we need a jolt to get us to make the change."

"Do you have unhealthy attachments?" I stared at him as I said this.

He held my gaze. "I do. Opening my ashrams ten years ago and this retreat five years ago helped to let go many of them as I retreated from the world and helped others along the way. But I still have some attachments to let go in this life."

Like Dee?

But I never uttered what was on my mind. Instead, I rose. I felt like Sisyphus on his uphill journey. "You've given me a lot to consider. I came out here thinking I could get away from my troubles. Instead you've placed them front and centre for me."

"Yes. And the only way is forward and through. Not around and away from, because troubles catch up again."

When I walked back to my cabin, the sun was setting over the lake, and I paused to soak it in. Such a peaceful setting, and I had foregone so many sunsets by locking myself in a downtown apartment to write tomes that had not mattered an iota to the world. I returned to my cabin and continued to cry.

At dinner that night everyone was upbeat except for me. I let the playful banter waft over me. The Davises were talking about their mastery of the canoe that had enabled them to reach the northern shore of the lake and find turtle eggs; Professor Darlington talked about three new bird categories he had seen and recorded during the day that were going into his bird-watching log which had 280 varieties logged for this year alone; Dee spoke about her ability to break away from pure-play landscapes and add human images, two lovers holding hands against a lake backdrop, a first for her in a long time. I was expecting the professor to eyeball me, and he didn't disappoint.

"And what masterpiece did our writer friend come up with today?" he asked, puffing on his pipe as we settled back from another splendid vegetarian repast that I had not done justice to despite my growling stomach.

"Revision," I replied.

"Oh." That stumped him, and I didn't elucidate.

The guru quickly interrupted with an announcement. "As tomorrow night will be your last night before we conclude the week, we will have a bonfire on the beach and dinner will be a barbecue."

"How do you have a vegetarian barbecue?" Marge Davis asked.

"My cook has found ingenious ways to harmonize the western tradition of barbecue with many eastern vegetarian dishes. Wild tandoori cauliflower, aubergine meze, paneer skewers, and vegan burgers, among others. You will not be disappointed."

As we broke up to return to our cabins, I avoided Dee's gaze. I guess she was expecting me to accompany her on the pathway like the previous night. But I hadn't spoken to her all day other than for meeting her on the doorstep of the guru's cabin, and in the state I was in I didn't want to interact with her tonight. I didn't want the disappointment of another walk down the proverbial and literal garden path with her.

As I headed towards my cabin, doubts plagued me. Should I have been that abrupt with her? Why was I becoming so pre-occupied with these people I had only met two days ago? Was it because I had for so long been only pre-occupied with fictional characters and hadn't engaged with real people? But these real people were exhausting me.

I sat on my deck and smoked a joint. Two in a day was a bit much for me. The lake was calm under a soft moon, but the weather report was calling for gusting winds later tonight. The loons were calling somewhere in the dark, goaded on by a dog's bark in the distance. Phil Davis came out on the deck with his wine glass filled to the brim. He sniffed, and I made no attempt to snuff out my toke. Then he grinned and raised his glass. "Cheers!"

I blew smoke. "Salut."

"Hey, we are going out to the north shore again tomorrow. Want to come along?"

"Sure." What the hell, it beat staring at a dead manuscript.

"Ten o'clock."

"If I'm awake."

I saw his wife sliding the deck door open and coming out with another full glass of wine in her hand.

"See you in the morning." I snuffed out my joint and flicked it away. I had no appetite for a wine and toke party with the Davises. "I've got to go to bed."

But sleep never came. The second joint had made me hyper, not calm. Long after the Davises had returned indoors, I tossed and turned and thought about Dee and kicked myself for having brushed her off. I should apologize. That's the problem. I had never apologized, not even to Susan for shutting myself away from her and depriving her of children and a normal married life. And now I was doing it again with another woman who had lit the only other spark in me.

I got out of bed and put on my running shoes. Slipping on a tee shirt, I left my cabin and walked over to Dee's. I took a circular path through the trees as I didn't want to give anyone the impression that I was prowling the resort at this hour. I would tap on her door, apologize for my behaviour and take what came, reward or punishment. I had taken enough punishment today. Let's see if I could put my trust in goodness for a change instead of cloaking humans with suspicion and ill will, like I did with my Victorian characters.

As I neared, I saw a light on in her cabin—good, she was still awake. But so was the light on in the professor's, which wasn't so good.

I was about to step out of the darkened woods into the illuminated path, when her door opened, and the guru emerged from within. He wore a saffron scarf over his white kantura. He swiped the scarf off his neck and hooked the person standing behind him with it, dragging Dee into his presence. Out she came into the circle of light on the threshold, a naked Dee whose nipples stuck out like daggers and whose lush pubic hair was a throwback to the '70's. I slunk back, deflated. Excited but deflated. The guru took a deep breath on the threshold and kissed her deeply, then puffed his chest like a man invigorated and proceeded down the path towards his cabin sans his scarf. Dee was transfixed in the light, and she seemed to be staring in my direction not in the guru's. But she couldn't see me, could she? I was still in the shadows. Then she withdrew abruptly and slammed the door, and the light went out in her cabin.

I fell back into the tree cover like I had been punched in the belly. The last sight I had of this sorry scene before I retreated to my cabin like a kicked dog was of the fluttering curtains in the professor's window before his cabin, too, settled into darkness.

I avoided everyone the next day. I even avoided my old manuscript and started to write a new piece. It was set in a naturist retreat. Everyone had to be naked in order to reveal their true selves. Before long, I was lost in this piece as the real people I had met at this resort started to emerge and merge with the characters in this new story, and I realized that I didn't have to use artifice or contrivance anymore. "Write about your own life," Susan had said. Well, I was finally attempting it. I just placed obstacles in the way of my characters, and, based on my knowledge of them, I got them to figure out their escape paths. I knew from the outset that I would never be able to sell this piece. Apart from the natural voyeurism of the reader wanting to look at people's naked bodies, there was no deep theme driving this story. No revolutions, no colonial conquests, no class battles, swordfights, or pistol duels, just a bunch of souls looking for enlightenment—boring! And yet...

By evening, I had written twenty-five pages, the most I had written in a day in a long time. What was more, I was looking forward to returning to this story as soon as I had another free moment to continue my engagement with its characters.

I dressed in tan slacks and a red floral shirt I had bought in Jamaica once, stuck my bare feet into sandals and went to dinner, hugging a pile of papers under my arm.

The dinner table was set on the beach and a huge bonfire provided heat and light. A barbecue was running beside it, from which delicious smells emanated. I was the last to arrive.

Dee wore the guru's saffron scarf over a white sheath dress that hugged her body—another throwback to an earlier age when she might have been slimmer, for every curve and bump in her figure was revealed. The others were deep in various discussions, with the Davis's slurring their words as usual. No one paid me any attention as I slunk into my seat. I dropped my pile of papers under my chair—that would come later. I looked over at Dee, but she had her head focussed on the table; she looked like she was contemplating something, something deep.

This meal was the best one I was to have at the resort during my stay. In addition to the staples of chappatis, alu gobi, paneer mataar, falafels and fragrant rice, there were barbecued meats: mutton kababs, chicken tikka and a beef shwarma dripping on a makeshift spit erected beside the barbecue.

The guru clapped his hands. "We do not forget that in this country you also eat meat. And as the key to good hospitality is making sure our guests are well looked after, we have catered to your non-vegan tastes as well. Please help yourselves."

The professor loaded his plate with meats, as if trying to make up for a week without any. The guru had none, neither did Dee. I ignored them and filled my plate with tiny morsels from each of the different dishes on offer. An arm reached across me, and I noticed Davis with a bottle of wine. "This helps the appetite. Want some?"

The guru was ignoring us, so I said, "Sure."

The wine felt good and loosened my inhibitions. Before long, we were all sweating, burping and farting as the food went down.

I held my glass out for a refill sometime during the meal, and Mrs. Davis winked as she fulfilled my request.

The guru stood up once to take a group photo of us eating.

As the meal was winding down, the wind began picking up according to the forecast. The guru stood to address us, his kaftan snapping dramatically.

"We should get to our renunciation ceremony before we are driven indoors by the weather. Tonight is when we get rid of old attachments. This is a purely voluntary exercise. Some of us are ready to give up, others not. There is no shame or stigma attached if you are unable to disassociate with your attachments. But this is your chance if you have reached such a conclusion." He sat down.

Dee stood up and unwound the saffron scarf from her neck. The guru gave her an alarmed look, and then kept his eyes focused on the table. I saw the professor reach for his camera.

Dee walked over to the bonfire, the wind and flames seeming to lick her figure in the body-hugging dress. She held the scarf over the fire, looked triumphantly towards the guru, and dropped the garment into the flames. "I renounce lust borne out of dependence."

The guru applauded, although his flapping hands made him look like he was sinking in one of the spruce bogs that dotted this area. "We must never be slaves to sex," he acquiesced. What the hell was he saying?

I heard the professor's camera click several times. Re-approaching the table, Dee stopped before the Professor, "And if any of my pictures from your camera get into social media or other public places, I will sue your ass off, Professor."

The professor flushed and Davis burst out laughing until both men were a deep purple. I thought it was my time before the wind blew out the fire.

The guru had risen and was holding up his camera. "But you don't mind if I take a photo, hah? Only for my album. It's not going on social media." I let him indulge himself.

Clutching the papers that I had retrieved from under my chair, I advanced upon the bonfire where I could now see only a burnt fragment of the saffron scarf remaining. Holding the pile above my head, I felt good about saying these words: "I discovered from an early stage in life that I was good at stringing words together. It saved my sanity when I was a teenager. And that was all I was good at. Then I tried to turn that gift into money by writing fiction, that is, lying for dollars. It has been an elusive journey, and I do not know who I am anymore. In the meantime, life was passing me by, and I was not recording any of it.

"Therefore, I hereby renounce my efforts at writing commercial fiction. If I ever write again, it will be about real people and the things that matter in their lives." I was to eat my words later, but right then it felt good saying it. I dropped the pile of papers into the middle of the bonfire where they could not be disturbed by the wind until they were reduced to embers.

Dee was standing and applauding. "Bravo!"

I blushed as I returned to my seat. Thankfully, Davis had refilled my glass of wine.

After a long pause, while everyone digested what had just gone on, the guru spoke again. "Is there anyone else who would like to renounce?"

"What about you, Swaminanda?" the professor shot back. "You're full of secrets and contradictions."

"I fed some of those contradictions, Professor," Dee interrupted. "Without a gullible and star-struck acolyte, the master cannot stray from the path."

The guru nodded his gratitude.

Davis drained the bottle into his glass. "Well, since I can't throw my useless kids into the fire, I'll drink to their speedy success at university and for their quick removal from my dependency list. Cheers!"

The guru stood. "Thank you all! Since there are no more renunciations, we should all go inside before the wind gets stronger—we could get embers from the fire coming our way soon."

Not long after I returned to my cabin the rain came down in buckets. Goaded by the wind, the outside world lapsed into a twilit haze. Isolated from the world, I picked up my new manuscript, my only available bed mate. I almost did not hear the tap on the front door.

Dee stood there in her shift, soaked to the skin. "Can I come in now?"

"Yes," I said, my breath catching. "But, with this rain, you might have difficulty getting back until the morning."

"I was not planning on leaving until the morning." She flipped off her dress and stood naked before me, arms outstretched.

When I awoke the following morning, I tried to recapture everything that had transpired. Not the coupling, but the cries as we experienced tender pleasure, the smells of our bodies, the tastes on our tongues. My commercial fiction had been full of people coupling, but what they tasted and felt, what they inhaled and imbibed of each other, I couldn't get to those places as my characters had lived in another time and sensibility. They were wooden, embalmed in history. But yesterday was wrapped around me like a musky cloak. Dee was all over me: in my mouth, in my nose, on my cock; her tongue had navigated hitherto taboo orifices in my body, taken samples and left her spoor behind in return. Last night would have to go into my new manuscript to make it real, like I had never been real before. Not only would it have depth, this new fiction would have texture. After months of searching, I had fallen into my next genre, the "something fresh" my agent had requested. Move over, Knausgaard!

She stirred and a whiff of morning breath wafted over. This prompted me to mount her again, and she playfully welcomed me, her strong legs pinning me from behind. This mounting game—she on me, me on her, just as strong as we felt the urge each time—had gone on all night in between periods of exhausted but buoyant slumber. This time the sound of our sexual satiation must have travelled far and wide along the row of cabins, for the rain had ceased.

After we finally rose and showered there was movement outside: I peered through a curtain while Dee put on her now dry shift.

"I seems like the Davises will not be canoeing after all," I said. "They are standing at the end of the dock. Their boat has lost its mooring and is drifting out on the lake."

"They should have renounced the boat last night. I guess Swami will have to ask the neighbour with the powerboat for a tow."

"Are we supposed to renounce each other? Is that what this is all about? Renounce desire?"

"No, we should be attracted to positive forces and renounce only negative ones. You are a positive force in my life. I felt it last night."

I reached out and kissed her. She was, indeed, in mine too. And right now, I did not want to contemplate expiry dates—there had been too many in my life. And I hadn't had a single nightmare yesterday—remarkable!

"Maybe I'll give you a ride back to the city today. That way we can get our co-ordinates—for future meetings, I mean."

"Sounds like a plan. Let's leave early before we become an item of interest. Before they start asking why we were screaming so loud in the storm."

I packed the car, wondering whether the old rust bucket would make it back in one piece, now that I had Dee and her luggage to lug as well. Well, it would be the time to test reliable Japanese engineering.

The guru walked over to us. "Ah, I see you have made a perfect union. Congratulations!" I scanned his face for sarcasm or bitterness, but there was only radiance. Perhaps I had really done him a favour by luring Dee away. Then panic hit me. Had he planted Dee on me? As a test for my next phase in life? Was that why it had all worked so easily last night with the naked Dee literally throwing herself at me?

Dee came around the side of the car and gave him a warm embrace, deepening my consternation. "Thank you very much, Swami. Thanks for everything."

"Go in peace, my dear." Then a thought occurred to him, and he turned to me. "Would you consider giving us an endorsement on our Facebook page?"

I felt like the commercial empire had reared its head and clobbered me on the face again—a parting shot as reward for renouncing commercialism last night. My face reddened and all thoughts that the guru was a deep man throwing tests in my way vanished. He was just a pedlar of his peculiar brand of product, flogging a meditation retreat while grabbing fringe benefits in the process. Puffing my chest, I asked, "Why are you bringing money back into this equation.? What happened to *Stuck in a Rut* and *Live in the Moment* and all those things that brought me here and cured me?"

The guru looked stunned at my outburst, then lowered his head. "You are right. A thousand pardons. I am right, too, when I said that I have some unwanted attachments that I still need to work through."

Not wanting him to wallow in his shame, we took our goodbye. "I'll like your Facebook page," I called out in parting and saw him brighten up.

As we meandered along the long driveway of the property to the main gate, Dee suddenly pointed. "There's the professor. I wondered what had happened to him in the storm." The professor was walking the path ahead of us, pausing occasionally to look for illusory birds.

We slowed as we neared him. He was bare bodied, in a baseball cap and khaki shorts; his sandals were as muddy as the soggy road. The camera had replaced the binoculars slinging from his neck.

"Bye, Professor," Dee said, winding the window down.

The professor stooped to peer into the car. "I see that you have found a quick replacement for your bedroom problem." The leering look on his face made me want to get out and punch him. But Dee laid a restraining hand on me.

"Sorry you see it that way, Professor," Dee replied. "We all come seeking, and we don't know what we will find until we realize it's what we have been looking for."

Her words were most re-assuring. Perhaps this would not end up a one-night stand after all. It couldn't. *Oh, God—it mustn't!*

"You came looking for birds, didn't you? And you found many new ones, too," Dee said to the professor.

"He came to 'out' the guru and his teaching," I added. "The birds were just a cover."

"Says the expert at snagging 'birds,'" the professor retorted, his voice rising. "I will expose this charlatan, Swaminanda, shortly. Watch the newspapers. I can also renounce things—and when I renounce, I make it complete, unlike you folks who don't renounce but swap one dependence for another."

"Try renouncing spying, Darlington. On women."

Darlington glared at me. Gone was the benign, academic look, replaced by cold steel in those eyes. "If the world goes in circles as the guru says, then we will meet again, Smallwood. If not, we won't."

"I think we should go," Dee whispered to me as she rolled up the window.

I accelerated, and the poor car responded with a groan that turned into a roar. I saw the professor looking bereft for being robbed of his moment of triumph. Then he took his camera and dashed it against a tree trunk. I hit the brake, and that too worked; the car slithered across the road and stopped. We both turned back to stare. Darlington didn't stop but kept banging the camera against the mighty wood until the instrument was a mess of broken metal and glass. Then he looked at us triumphantly, holding up the destroyed camera like a trophy.

I stepped on the gas again and didn't slow down until we were well on the main road. Japanese engineering had indeed not let us down.

"The problem is that I no longer know where this new fictional world ends and the real one begins," I said. "I feel like I am living inside a novel."

"And I can't tell the bad guys from the good ones," Dee said, settling in for the long ride back to Ottawa.

I kept glancing at her throughout the drive, as if expecting her to vanish like a fictional character in my imagination. After all, she *was* going to be intrinsic to my new fiction, to the next novel I was going to write.

Chapter 2

Dee and I dated for the next three months. She lived in Hull, and I had to drive across the bridge to visit her. I would rather make the trip to her house because my place was usually a mess: clothes that hadn't gone to the basement laundry, empty pizza cartons, books and magazines, and my squeeze balls that ended up in strange places. Once—and the only time she consented to have sex with me in my messy quarters—one lodged under her bum, just as I was about to enter through her portals of heaven. Pausing to remove the offending obstacle killed all spontaneity. We had to pause for a glass of wine before making another attempt.

Her digs were spartan by comparison: a studio apartment neatly arranged with canvases—not more than three on display at a time: her current work-in-progress, the previous one completed, and one that served to inspire her at present—a pull-out couch that was her bed, a tiny kitchenette, and a tinier bathroom. Life was cozy on that pull-out couch, and the sex was tight, and regular, with no hidden objects getting lodged in one's derriere.

I worked on my new novel during that time or tried to. But it floundered after the sex scenes dissipated. After all, Dee and I were just meeting to have sex. But the sex was good in one way for I never had my usual nightmares during that time with her. Sex was our substance. Sure, we tried going to the movies, but Netflix was cheaper, and then it became a battle for which one of the endless series on this binge channel to watch. I figured working in this new medium must be a writer's dream; one scene could be dragged out into a dozen episodes! This beat my former historical fiction, anytime. In fact, my new novel was becoming like a never-ending Netflix series, all it had was sex.

I think Dee was beginning to get this message too, for she started finding ways to cancel out on our daily couplings. Let's face it, I wasn't the greatest guy in the sack, and she was so much sexier she could have a lineup of guys.

"Why don't you check out a lineup of guys?" I once asked after she had come twice in the same evening, and I had just pleaded for a reprieve from trying to grow a third horn in as many hours.

She giggled and snuggled up to me, her heavy musk helping coax my flagging protuberance into renewed excitement. "You're faithful. And I like you." She kissed me deeply, and I was up and inside her in a flash.

But I knew that passion would abate, and when she kept reminding me of the upcoming appointment with an agent who was interested in her work and wanted to commission a job from her, and that this would be followed with some meetings in Toronto where the client was located, I realized she was trying to tone us down. I wondered jealously whether the agent was the first in that lineup of guys.

"I thought you had quit the corporate business?" I asked sneakily, trying to ferret out more.

"Following your dream is fine, but it's not paying any bills. This gig is different. Bill. . .the agent. . .wants more of what I'm presently doing, with one or two modifications. You could say it's a happy compromise between doing what you want and doing what others want."

"They'll stifle you."

"If shaving my armpits and legs to conform to boardroom standards is stifling, I guess so. Oh darn, I guess I'll have to get back into a regular grooming routine soon."

And so, Dee, fully groomed, kept her appointment with her agent and the client, and I tried to work on my novel but gave it up and masturbated instead—this was the first evening in three months that I had not had sex. Not bad for a guy who had been on the celibacy wagon for months at a time before that. Now I couldn't get by an evening on my own. Then I watched Netflix, and the movie *I wanted*, not one of those never-ending series shows where all I could think about was its scriptwriter reeling the dough in. Later I smoked a toke to drown out feelings of inadequacy and jealousy. I even cried that night.

Dee called me the following morning. She was almost shouting over the phone. "They bought it! They want six paintings in two months for their new corporate headquarters, with themes of realizing dreams, teamwork and vision."

"The executive suite hasn't changed much has it?"

"But the mandate is broad this time, I get to choose how to represent those buzzwords."

"Two months. That's three a month. I'll never see you."

Her voice took a conciliatory tone. "Don't say that. We will still meet. But not that often."

"I want to see you every day."

"That won't happen unless we live together. How about once a week and on weekends?"

"What? That's starvation diet."

"That's more sex than most people get. Ask the politicians who throng this town from all over the country. They even try cheap hook-ups via Twitter."

"Are you accepting invitations from them too?" I couldn't get the sarcasm out of my voice, and she got curt.

"Will—watch your tone. You are starting to sound like a spoiled kid who had his candy taken away."

"Sorry. All the best with the new assignment. I know you will do a great job." I was already resolving to increase my shifts at the supermarket.

"Thanks. I have something that you might be interested in. Those politicos you so easily denigrate, well, one of them happens to be a second cousin twice removed. He needs a social media blurb writer. I mentioned you."

"What?" I guess this is where I need to pause and ask myself why the heck I had never considered becoming a speech writer, policy paper writer, translator or any one of those armies of hacks in the nation's capital, the mecca for script writers, who were paid by the word by a myriad of government offices, bureaus and agencies that dotted this city. Why? Because I had always considered myself above them. I was a *creative* writer. I wrote my own shit, not someone else's. I was not a recorder; I was a generator.

But now I paused at her words. Back-breaking extra shifts at the supermarket, or easy money for typing some useless text when my novel refused to budge? And the offer was coming from the woman who was beginning to drift away from me.

"What do I need to do?" I said, taking a deep breath and damning my soul to Hades for this capitulation.

I reported to the office of the cousin twice removed the following day, an obscure third floor office in a nondescript building behind the ByWard Market. The cousin was not in; he was visiting his riding, the receptionist told me, but Mr. Darlington, his communications director, would see me. At mention of the name my ears pricked up. It couldn't be. . .no, that had to be a coincidence, perhaps that image of a smashed camera on a country road was just too vivid. . .

But it was.

The tall man who lunged with alacrity from behind his small desk was none other than Professor Darlington of the not-so-distant past.

"Ah, Smallwood. Nice to see you again. The world is indeed circulatory." His manner was cordial and blustery. Our friction at the resort was either forgotten, or it may not have even happened.

"Professor Darlington. I didn't know you worked here."

"Oh, I split my time between the university and government, you see. This is a consulting engagement for me." I found out later that his contract had not been renewed at the university in Toronto for the coming school year.

"I understand that there is a job for a script writer for the web."

"Yes. Our ministry interfaces a lot with the public over the environment, and the minister hired me to run his media campaign."

And you hire me to do it for you. I decided not to be cheeky and looked interested instead. "Sounds like a very important assignment." I looked around the room, taking in the shabby desks facing each other, one for the professor and one for his secretary who appeared to be ignoring us but revealed her inquisitiveness with her forward posture and one ear turned in our direction. The rest of the room was a jumble of files, filing cabinets, a fax machine, and a percolator with dregs of stale coffee that I wasn't offered.

Darlington remained standing as he expanded on the job with his hands outstretched. "Yes—we are getting slammed a lot about the carbon tax issue, and the pipelines, and the Paris Accord, and we need to have sustained pieces in social media that alter the public perception of our inactivity, or, pardon my candour, inefficiency in these areas. By the way, did you see my op-ed on Swaminanda?"

I had been so busy having sex and writing a new type of novel, I hadn't been paying much attention to the gossip columns. "Er…I'm afraid I haven't."

"You have to keep up, you know. In this job you will be expected to read all the dailies and the weeklies and the monthly journals, not forgetting to keep tabs on what's trending on Facebook and Twitter and all those other online forums."

"Sounds like a twenty-four seven assignment. How much does it pay?"

"Well, you will be paid by the piece you write."

"So, I don't get paid for all the reading up of trends that I will have to do?"

"No. But you need to do that in order to write the pieces we commission you to write."

"What did you say about Guru Swaminanda?"

The professor reached behind his desk and snatched out a newspaper. It must have been lying there for display to all and sundry, not just me. It was in the Lifestyle section of a national newspaper; the headline was enough to warn me: *Self-Discovery Retreats—the latest gold rush.*

I scanned the first few paragraphs out of courtesy to my job interviewer. The article, written in rather academic language, went on to castigate middle-class westerners who fell for snake oil salesmen selling ephemeral happiness. "…Meditation stills the mind and neuters the imagination…intellectual discourse is discouraged…nothing in the eastern arts can be scientifically proven…" At the bottom of the article there was a mention of the author going to a retreat and its location—enough to black ball Swaminanda without resorting to libel. I looked up from the newspaper.

"Quite damning," I said. "By the way, Dee and I are still together three months on. That was not ephemeral." At this point I didn't care whether I got this job or not. I wanted to beat this arsehole's face just like he had beaten that hapless camera.

His face reddened. He gulped and tried to regain his composure. "My congratulations to you both. It was indeed out of courtesy to her that the minister asked me to dispense with the usual hiring process and bring you on board, given this is only a minor contract position. I thought that was rather grand."

And more ammunition in your crusader's gun should this job sour and you decide to take on the mismanagement in government next. But I merely smiled.

"Yes, it would be grand to work with you." He smiled. "You realize of course that if your work is not up to snuff, you will be fired forthwith?"

"A writer is used to rejection. Yes, I am aware of the penalties for non-performance."

"You will send in all your pieces to me for review before they are posted. Our secretary, Maddie here, will set you up with logins and other things you need to get started. We will probably communicate by e-mail most of the time as I will be on the road a lot for the minister."

"Sounds good to me. I take it I can also work from home, as I have other commitments to deal with."

"Of course. The lovely Divine Secrets being one, I am sure. Besides, we don't have a desk here for you. As you can see, our quarters are quite cramped." To emphasise this, he sat down again, and his knees lifted the desk between us.

"I'm sure the less we see of each other the more successful we will be at this job," I said and saw Maddie suppress a laugh that she turned into a mild cough, while Darlington went red again.

"Yes, it will indeed be grand working with you, Smallwood," was all he could manage. The phone on his desk rang, and he grabbed it, saying, "Good morning, minister."

I knew our interview was over but that I had been appointed to a government job. I turned over to the smiling Maddie, who looked more inviting than her boss, to get the logistics attended to.

I phoned Dee as soon as I stepped out of the office. "Guess who's my boss?" When I revealed his identity to her, she burst out laughing. Then she turned serious.

"It's true what the guru told me, then."

"Darlington calls our guru a gold digger in his exposé," I said.

Dee carried on as if ignoring me. "We keep running into the same people in different roles until we learn the lessons they are supposed to teach us. That's what Guru Swaminanda told me."

"You think my running into Darlington again was pre-ordained?"

"It's creepy. Did you get the job?"

"Yes, but I don't know how long I will last."

"I can't help you there. I can only open doors."

"Will you open your door to me tonight? We could celebrate the new job."

"Mine or yours?"

"Both. No, let's do yours first. Then mine, if I last through the week."

"Okay. You are twisting my arm. This once-a-week business is not working out."

"It should be flexible when special occasions come up."

"See you at eight o'clock."

"Why so late?"

"I'm attending a corporate ethics seminar from four to seven p.m."

"What on earth for?"

"If I am going to be representing and projecting the corporation in my work then I had better know what they stand for."

"I could have told you. 'Buy low, sell high, exploit your employees and salt away the profits'—simple."

We ate at a quiet family-run Italian trattoria that evening, a rare occasion, for on most days we were balancing weekly pay cheques, opting to cook indoors or have takeout. Today we were eating against earnings still to materialize. It was like taking out our first mortgage together. I drank a bit too much wine; we both did.

We staggered home—hers—and fell onto the pull-out couch, that wasn't even pulled out—we settled for the rug. Later, as I rubbed ointment on the carpet burns on her knees, I said, "You know Dee, I think I am in love with you."

She raised her head and stuck her tongue out at me. I kissed her tongue, and it felt good. It felt good opening up.

"Are you going to put this scene in your book too?" she asked, limping over to her dresser to pull on a pair of pyjamas.

She had hit a sore point, for I gushed in an anguish that must have been lurking somewhere. "That's the problem—I don't know you. All I can write about is what we do in the moment and that makes it one step removed from an erotica novel. I don't know your early life. Were you married before, do you have parents alive, brothers, sisters? Where were you born? We are strangers outside the sack."

From the bottom of the dresser she pulled out a weathered, leather covered album. She returned and sat by me.

"Okay, let me tell you," she began...

"Daddy—he was my step-father, actually—was my whole life. My biological father died of a boating accident when I was a year old, and my mother married his best friend who had been on that same boat. A kind of fatal attraction. My step-father, therefore, Daddy, as I called him, was also my nemesis," Dee said fingering the sepia photograph of a tall man with a shock of dark hair and a pencil moustache, muscles rippling under a white shirt and tie. The man was helping a little girl in a pinafore on a bicycle.

"Is that you on the bike?" I asked.

"On my tenth birthday. Daddy gave me the bicycle as a present. He had money. A tenured professor of English."

"And your mother?"

She fished out another photograph. A retiring petite woman, as if reluctant to pose for the camera, blonde stringy hair, aquiline nose, wearing a long dark dress, her head slightly averted from the camera. "Mom was the painter who never made it. She painted until arthritis got in the way. The more Daddy played around, the more she painted. Even their heights were incompatible. Perhaps opposites attracted, for awhile."

I sat back. I knew this was going to be a painful story.

Dee was an only child. Her mother had suffered a prolapsed womb after Dee was born. There were rumours that Daddy had many girlfriends: university faculty, even students. But he never brought any of his sins home, so life had been fine, idyllic. Daddy doted on Dee, while her mother had become more withdrawn and reserved, shunning attendance at faculty parties and dances that were the normal social circles for academics.

"Then one day, Daddy was suspended. For alleged sexual abuse of one of the first-year students. It was a terrible time. He became depressed. My parents were sleeping in separate bedrooms at that time, and I saw him suffering every day. I was fourteen and was in the full bloom of puberty. One day, when Mum was out, he came to my room. . ."

"Oh, no—not one of those. . ." I held my head.

"Yes, unfortunately. At first it was fondling. It was very loving. He was in pain, and I wanted to comfort him. Then he got bolder and started to make me nervous."

"I'm sorry. Men are horrible creatures."

"He swore me to secrecy. Said that Mom would leave if she found out. I didn't want my world that had been the two of them from the day I was born splitting apart. Besides, he was so mournful when he caressed my body, as if he was searching for something lost. So, I shut my mouth and allowed him to continue his 'ministrations'. After awhile I got used to it and began to relax. And I began to like it too. It was our secret, Daddy's and mine."

It ended badly. Her mother caught them *in flagrante delicto* one day.

"It was bound to happen." Dee sighed. "I was sent to live with my mother's sister who had a family of four children. My parents went through the motions of counselling but that fell apart when my step-father was fired from the university after the investigation concluded that he had committed a string of sexual violations, not just the one that had started his slide."

Dee's parents' marriage ended then too.

"Daddy visited me at my aunt's and promised to look after me. I asked him to take me away with him as I hated my cousins and my aunt even more. His ministrations were preferable to their bullying. But Mom wouldn't have it. Dad got a job out west in the oil fields and sent me money from time to time. After awhile I left my aunt's and went to live with Mom, but she was a bitter woman who blamed me for all that had happened between her and Daddy. When I was seventeen, I left home. Daddy paid for my art school, but I haven't seen either of them since."

"And so endeth another stereotypical tale of happy Canadian family life, replete with its brooding dark secrets," I said, rising and walking over to the window. Dee put away the photo album. Her story was so reminiscent of another one I knew but couldn't talk about.

"Now you can tell me your story," she said, "since we are into all this revealing."

I was dreading the moment. My story was more complicated. I did not want to be relegated to being a deadbeat. But I was a deadbeat. Dee's step-father had done better than I had done, despite his groping and crossing moral boundaries.

"Tomorrow," I said. "I've had a lot to absorb tonight. You've been through a lot."

Dee came and sat beside me. She took my hand. "That's why I believe in circular interactions in life. What goes around comes around and all that. It's because of my step-father that I am drawn to mentor-types like Swaminanda, why I defer to perverts like Darlington because of their professorial bearing."

"How does that account for people like me?"

"You are the artist in me. The one my mother aspired to become but couldn't. This unfulfilled quest ultimately became the source of her resentment. You represent the grail that we all seek, the impossible dream."

"Now, hold on. I am no hero. I have not achieved the literary pinnacle by any stretch of anyone's imagination."

"That's precisely it—you are trying to reach for it—that undiscovered country, in your new form of writing. Will you reach it? Who knows? But you are reaching upwards. That's attractive in a man."

I pondered that. "Hmm. That helps. Gives me a reason to get up in the morning." I kissed her.

I read up a lot on writing for social media over the next few days, and it was overwhelming. There were times I thought of bowing out. Then I remembered the Netflix screenwriters. They too must have come from traditional grounds and had to adapt; now they were raking it in. Adapt or die. So, I plodded on. I sent three blog articles, five Facebook posts and ten tweets over to Darlington after three days of assiduous "social media for dummies" study. I got the following response back in a detailed e-mail:

My dear Smallwood,

Can you answer me the following:

1) Why do you repeat the same word so many times?

2) Why are your paragraphs so short? They read like a dime novel. Our readers are more educated than that, you know.

3) What are these hashtags for? Why so many? Are they congruent with our audiences?

4) Why are you adding all these pictures and links to other sites? Our message will get lost the moment the reader clicks to go elsewhere.

I had to conclude that the honorable minister had hired a dummy for a consultant. Darlington was a college professor from the Mesozoic era. At least, from before computers were invented. And pre-internet, for sure. Biting my feeling of wanting to tell him to bite his cock and die, I explained, in not too biting language, in an e-mail that I composed back to him, that the recommendation from social media experts was that short sentences held attention spans that were shrinking today. So did pictures over text. The links to related sites I had inserted opened on to separate web pages, so readers did not leave our page. Word repetition helped with Search Engine Optimization. Then I scratched out the acronym SEO and just wrote "Google can find us better." I concluded by saying that if these posts didn't go up today, they would be obsolete tomorrow, and we would have to come up with a new crop—rapid obsolescence was endemic in social media. I let him chew on it. Two hours later, I got a curt reply: "Post them."

Things got better after that. Darlington stayed out of my way for the most part. He sent me just the important issues of the day, asked me to read up on developments in our ministry and on the environment in general, and then blog and tweet about them and respond to tweets from the public. After awhile, I wondered whether I had totally gained his trust and confidence or whether he was hiding his ignorance from me, for he stopped asking to review my articles before they were posted. I worried that it was going to be a matter of time before I overstepped my bounds and brought the wrath of the ministry upon my head. Perhaps Darlington was avoiding me in the hope that I would self-destruct.

I was also avoiding my own unravelling to Dee. I had not called her the day after our "celebration" and had not visited during the entire working week. I sent her a text and feigned the challenge of getting to grips with this social media beast as the reason for my pre-occupation and absence. For the first time, it was me who was avoiding our meetings, or couplings. But I knew that I was running away from my past, not the past with Susan, but the one that had come before, the one that even Susan knew nothing about.

Could I import that past into my new novel? The guys on Netflix did it all the time, flashbacks within flashbacks until the audience gives up and goes with the flow, trusting that the scriptwriter will get them to the final destination. But that past would turn my novel from a love story into a farce. Or at least a story of betrayal, where the protagonist, me, would be relegated to being unreliable, un-heroic, and un-relatable. Would that fly? Would this end up being my confessional novel, where in its writing I would be making peace with myself and damn everyone else?

At the spiritual retreat I had given up my traditional formulaic novel writing. I had sworn to tell the truth going forward, warts and all. Why was I holding back then? Shouldn't I tell Dee the truth? She had been so forthcoming with me and revealed her painful past. She would understand if I told her my story. And yet...

It was on the Friday of that week when the guru's theory of circular relationships was brought home to me. I received a tweet response to my tweet about an innocuous ministry initiative on the Great Lakes. *You treat humans, especially your family, less importantly than you treat the fish in the lakes.* The tweeter had the handle @abandonedchild97.

This rankled a nerve. Why should this constituent, this tweeter, even if from the opposition, become so personal? Were they aiming this barb at the minister? Surely, he or she couldn't be targeting me for I was an anonymous writer for hire. But I was intrigued because the nerve it was pinching was too close to me at the moment.

I went into my personal Twitter account—big mistake—and to my surprise found that the account was following me there too. I followed them back to make the connection and messaged them. *Why are you pissed off with the Ministry of the Environment?*

The response was instantaneous: *I am pissed off at YOU. I know who you are, Mr Scriptwriter.*

My flesh crawled. Cut this exchange off now or proceed? I proceeded.

There's a whole department of us, I replied. Let that confuse the poor asshole.

You are nothing but a deserter. A deadbeat. And I'm coming for you.

I was sweating now. Of course, this guy could track me down. Should I unfollow and block them? Something said that I shouldn't. This was a vital link with something in my past, and I couldn't let it go. I tried to put things in perspective: I was the whole of Darlington's social media department. Was it Darlington himself having some fun at my expense and trying to unsettle me? Was the ministry auditing me? Why the hell had I switched over to my personal account? Guilt? I discontinued the tweet exchange and logged back into the ministry accounts.

That same afternoon, after posting my official blogs, tweets and other social media blurbs, and shutting off all devices that I may have left a footprint on, I took a walk down to the canal. Snow was beginning to fall on this mid-November day, and the water was flowing sluggishly. People were bundled up, rushing by to buses, cars or the nearest shopping arcade to get out of the chilly wind. Others huddled in shelters waiting anxiously for their destination bus numbers to arrive. I headed down the steps of Portage Bridge into Victoria Island Park and took the footpath. I was supposed to meet Dee in an hour, and I needed the time to compose myself for our meeting.

I dusted off the snow from a park bench and sat down. I was the only soul out here as the snow was falling in larger accumulations; pedestrians on the bridge were disappearing in the whiteness enveloping everything. I felt safe, cocooned by the snow; even that mad tweeter wouldn't find me here. It had been on a snowy day like this twenty-one years ago when I had met her. Jacqueline.

Chapter 3

I met Jacqueline in a bar when I was finishing my English degree. She was carrying six flagons of beer on a tray, hands raised overhead, expertly navigating the shouting patrons and a few grabby old men who were reaching for the tankards, hoping to miss and land on her generous breasts instead.

When she passed me, she shouted, "What's yours?"

"I'll have one of those, whatever."

"Coming up, next round." Then she was back behind the bar, jerking the taps and filling up more beer. I bet the grabby old men were wishing to trade in their cocks for those one-arm bandits. It was Reading Week and freezing outside, snow grabbing the windows and staying put while patrons, mainly students from the nearby campus with a sprinkling of those randy retired fellows, were huddled around tables guzzling the only booze they could afford, beer.

I paused from my work to admire this new server: a tight white tee shirt with a few splotches of sweat in intimate places, curvy hips swirling under snug denims, and a shock of black hair that she tossed back effortlessly as she served the thirsty masses mewling around her. I lost interest in my work.

Work was also a way of escaping my nightmares. I had just discovered that when I poured my imagination into writing and went home exhausted, I slept relatively peacefully. I had tried all the others: counselling, medication and pot; none worked as effectively as writing.

"Molson Draft!" The new server dropped a frosty pint on my table without sloshing a drop. "I'll take cash now as I am busy, and some people leave without paying."

As I reached for my wallet, she stared at my laptop, bending closer. I could smell shampoo and strong deodorant. "That's sounds pretty fancy for a university thesis. People cutting off heads!"

"Don't pry. It's my masterpiece, my debut novel. When it sells, I won't be hanging out in hovels like this."

"Ha! Thy ambition knows no bounds, my lord!" She made such a theatrical bow, I couldn't help but enquire.

"Ryerson, School of Drama," she replied, cheerfully.

"Congratulations. When do you graduate?"

"This summer."

"That makes two of us."

There was an energy radiating from her that made me forget work. I wanted to talk to her and not let her get back behind that bar. She held the energy of the room, as if everyone depended on her to keep them alive at their tables to engage in conversation and drink.

"I guess, now that we've met, I am supposed to ask you out for a drink after work. But I must be standing in line with everyone else in this room."

"I haven't said 'yes' to anyone, yet." She pulled a cloth out of her jeans pocket and swiftly wiped down my table where I had swilled beer in my excitement.

"A drink then. What time do you get off?" I tried to keep my hands from shaking.

"It's reading week for me. Sorry. I'm in a term-end play and the scouts from Stratford are coming."

I was deflated. I had sensed it wasn't going to be this easy and turned back to my historical fiction novel on the laptop. I was just at the part where the hero, a French *citoyen* grabs the bourgeoisie woman to show her just who is master, now that *La Revolution* had upended the social order. I could hear her giggle.

"Try me on Friday," she whispered.

"I don't come here on Fridays."

"I saw you here last week Friday?"

It was true. But how the heck did she know?

"Have you been spying on me?"

"No, but I was off duty and having a drink with some of my cast friends over by the other corner when I saw you come in and open your laptop. A man with a laptop in a room full of drunken people stands out."

I raised my glass to her, relief rushing out like gas from an opened beer bottle. "*Salut.* To next Friday, then." Smiling, she was off, tossing that black mane behind her, wriggling her hips and grabbing the taps behind the bar to yank out more frothing suds.

That's how Jacqueline and I met. Our second meeting was different. We met at the bar and walked down to a bistro across the park from the university, on her side of town. She shed her coat as soon as we got a table. Underneath, she was wearing a slinky white top that accentuated her cleavage, making me break out in a sweat. Her makeup was elaborate with eyeliner drawing out eyelashes like an Elphaba. Was that her new part in the end of term play? I didn't have to wait long to find out about the femme fatale look. Over our first drink, she looked cautiously around her, pulled out a pouch, and slipped a pill from it into her glass.

"What the doctor ordered?" I asked cautiously.

"Bennies. I need them for my mental balance. Want one?"

"No thanks!"

She shoved the pouch at me. "Go on. Don't be a square."

"Do you take downers after that too?"

"Life is a downer. I don't need downers. Work in a bar and struggle with men pawing you all the time—that's a downer. Then your director wants to screw you in exchange for a plum part in the play. Want more downers?"

I took one of the black and orange capsules out of the pouch. The grains inside the transparent half of the pill looked like cancerous pustules. I downed my drink. After the second drink, with my apprehensions drowned, I dropped the bennie into my third round.

Jacqueline got more ebullient as the evening progressed. She told me about her mother, also an actress, who had to quit her career to look after Jacqueline after getting pregnant by a married theatre producer.

"I'm going to do better than Mom, who cursed me from the day I was born," she said, knocking her drink back and signalling the server for another.

"Do you keep in touch?"

"No. She moved to L.A. when I was seventeen. Lives with a musician. Still hopes for a comeback, but all she does is sell curios in a tourist shop on Hollywood Boulevard."

"And your father?"

"How do you think I got into drama school? Nepotism helps." She tossed her hair back and laughed.

"Do you see him?"

"No, but he pays my way. Took over as soon as Mom decamped— but at a distance. E-mail and the odd phone call work for him. He has a family that he doesn't want to compromise with me being in the picture."

We ordered food, but she just picked at it, intent more in talking and swaying gently in her chair to the background music. Her eyes were luminous, dreamy. I was melting inside them.

Then she started to loom larger at me, and I was developing an itch on my cock. It must have been the bennie. She grinned, looking at my face. "Are you horny yet?"

"How did you know?"

"I'm there already. I've been waiting for you to catch up. Very soon this bus will leave the station."

Before we left any stations I had to ask the question that had been foremost in my mind all evening. "Why did you choose to hang out with me?"

"Because you don't look like an opportunist. You are too self-absorbed and serious."

Then I said something I had never been bold enough to say to a girl before. "Then let's get out of here."

She grabbed her coat. "My apartment is just around the corner. And my roommate is working the night shift today."

We fornicated like crazy that night. I can't remember getting into her little one-bedroom apartment that had a curtain strung across the living room—her roomie's bedroom, she later told me. She smoked a joint while we hurried, nay ran over to her place; I got the last couple of puffs before we entered the building and ran up the stairs to the fourth floor, ignoring the elevator that sometimes didn't work.

She pulled me into her bedroom, the one with a door. It only had room for a queen-sized bed. I gave up observations at that point and focussed on my lust that had mounted to bursting point. Her breath was warm on my body; her tongue seeking, devouring, enveloping me; her need insistent. "Fuck me" was all I heard during our intense entanglement on her unmade bed, in this room that smelled of patchouli. Later, we stretched in the knotted bed sheets, breathing in each other's sweaty passion until it re-awakened us to repeat our performance again and again, until we both passed out in exhaustion and the come-down from the drug.

I jerked awake at eight a.m. from a dreamless sleep. My head felt like it would explode, and my mouth was dry. I also noticed that my cock had not worn a condom in the heat of our passion; pausing for that act of hygiene would have been a downer, and Jacqueline didn't need downers she'd said.

I heard sounds in the living room. Then the door opened and a shaved male head sporting an earring poked inside.

"Hey!" I yelled in panic, pulling the bed sheets over my nakedness.

"I'm Tom. It's okay." The voice was effeminate, affected. "I'm her roomie." The man eased himself into the room sideways through the door crack. He was scrawny and tall. He lifted Jacqueline's panties off the floor, held it to his nose, and wrinkled his features. "That one's for the laundry." He tossed it in a basket in a corner that held other used clothes.

"Would you mind?" I said, getting a bit annoyed. Beside me, Jacqueline snored hard.

Tom waved a hand in front of his face, dismissively. "Oh, don't worry. I don't go for her gender. That's why we are roomies. We look out for each other. And keep yourself covered or I might go for you."

He appraised the sleeping woman and shook his head. "She mustn't take those uppers all the time, especially now that she is approaching graduation. I worry for her." He knelt on the other side of the bed and stroked her hair.

I felt guilty. I reached for my underpants that had landed on a pile of books beside the bed and put them on under the sheet. I didn't want Tom to have a go at me. With my crotch covered, I arose and started to dress.

"I'll get the coffee," Tom said and tiptoed out of the room.

Jacqueline stirred and rubbed her eyes. She dragged herself up into a sitting position, a yawn breaking out and the bed sheet falling off to reveal her perfect breasts that I had feasted on not too long ago. A wave of desire coursed through me again, but I held off from acting upon it. Then I saw the rings around her eyes as she removed her hands from rubbing them. She had her chin down, and her eyes stared up at me, the residue of the Elphaba makeup made her look like Cruella de Ville now.

"What are you still doing here?" she shot out, and the edge in her voice startled me.

"I...er...slept over. In case you didn't recall," I said, feeling insulted at this outburst. Had she forgotten me already?

"You were supposed to have fucked and gone. No one sees me the morning after." The door opened and Tom arrived carrying a tray with two steaming coffee mugs. "Except Tom."

Tom winked at me and offered me a mug. I grabbed it like it was a lifesaver. Then he returned to Jacqueline and placed the other cup in her hands, cradled them and moved the mug towards her lips. "Wakey, wakey..." he cooed.

She drank like a lost traveller finding water at a desert oasis, greedily, with driblets of coffee escaping and dripping off the sides of her mouth. Tom wiped off the spillage with a napkin that he had slung over his shoulder. I guess he knew the drill around here. When Tom retrieved the cup from her, tears flowed out of her eyes. Soon she was sobbing, her chest heaving, as if some deep sorrow was trying to escape. Tom held her by the shoulders, casting an anxious glance at me, suggesting that I had better leave now. But I wanted to stay. I wanted to do what Tom was doing. I wanted to comfort her.

He laid her back on the bed again and pulled the sheet over her. He stroked her head. "It's the weekend, honey. Get some rest. I'm off for some winks too."

Sleep after coffee? What was he smoking? But within moments, she was snoring contentedly again. Tom gestured for me to leave the room with him. I complied.

Outside in the partitioned living room, he said, "She'll sleep until about six p.m. I slipped a Quaalude into her coffee. She'll be better when she wakes the next time."

"Is she like this normally?"

"She's Bipolar. She manages to keep herself balanced with medication. She must have had some emotional turbulence last night that upset the balance." Tom looked worried. "I hope that wasn't you?"

I shrugged. I didn't know what to say. He showed me out.

As I exited the apartment, I couldn't help but feel that I wasn't just one of Jacqueline's other joes who "fucked and left" and that I had caused her enough turbulence to turn her emotions into jelly. As much as it was a horrible thought, I had to say there was a bounce in my step all the way home.

The next day I sat in the back row of the university's almost empty theatre and watched her play the lead in a rehearsal of *Medea*, the end of term play. She didn't know I was there, and I had to do some sleuthing and lying to get admitted into the theatre. But by now I was obsessed with her. And as I watched her switch from spurned bride to avenging woman, I saw the shapeshifting that had taken place in her apartment happen again. She ranted, grovelled, strode across the stage, then crawled back the other way; her immersion in the role was total. The rest of the cast, particularly the guy playing husband, Jason, were wooden in comparison to Jacqueline.

When Medea returns from off-stage to announce that she has killed their children to avenge Jason's betrayal, her lines, delivered in a deliberate metronomic beat, made my skin crawl.

I wouldn't want to be in the bad books of this Medea.

When the show ended, a man in the front row walked up to the proscenium, clapping. He said something to the bowing Medea, and she clutched her hands with glee.

I waited at the exit from the green rooms until she came out. She paused on seeing me, then rushed over and gripped my hands as if nothing untoward had happened between us. "Did you watch the show?" Her eyes were wide in expectation.

"You were fabulous."

She giggled. "That's exactly what Mr. Perrault said afterwards."

"You mean as in Ross Perrault, the producer guy?"

"Yes. He's a friend of my father. He wants me to try out for *Miss Julie* this fall. The show is going to play at Niagara in the spring."

"That's great." I didn't know anything about Strindberg or his plays at the time. "Shall we grab a bite? You can educate me on *Miss Julie*. Hope she is as dastardly as Medea."

She looked at her watch. "No, I have to meet with Mr. Perrault at his suite at the Royal Excelsior. He is in town only tonight before he heads off to New York tomorrow."

Seeing the disappointment on my face, she touched my hand. "I know I was awful to you yesterday. I can't help it. Things just happen that way. I try to make it work for me, in the acting and all. But it creeps into real life."

"It's okay. Maybe I'll wait for you after your meeting with Perrault."

Her face clouded over. "No. I don't want to be on a clock. This is the biggest opportunity for me to break into the mainstream, and I want to give Mr. Perrault all the time he needs."

My bitterness was mounting at the thought of her in the hotel suite of a famous theatrical producer with the flowing blond mane, known for his much-publicized sexual peccadilloes that kept the *National Enquirer* in business. That he was her father's friend made no difference to a man with a randy cock.

She touched me again, a bit more insistently. "Don't worry. I know how to look after myself. And I can't screw this up."

I walked her to the subway, and after she had taken the streetcar, I took a taxi and arrived at the Royal Excelsior ahead of her. I saw her enter the lobby and take the elevator. I walked into the lobby bar and nursed a drink. I waited three hours for her to come out of those elevator doors, the number of drinks mounting with my disappointment. Finally, I realized that I was too drunk to meet her if she came out now and took myself home.

I didn't hide my jealousy when we next met, which was two days later at the pub where she worked. I waited until she had a break and asked to talk to her in the alleyway.

"You were fucking him!" I came to the point, spitting out my anger and disgust.

"No way!"

"What were you doing in his suite for three hours, maybe longer?"

"We weren't there. He invited me to dinner, and we took the elevators on the York Street side to go to the sea food restaurant across the street. After dinner, he ordered a cab to take me home. Besides, who gives you control of me? We've only met a couple of times."

I was floored like that Jason character in her play. I felt her drifting away from me, and I couldn't let her go. I grabbed her and pulled her to me. I kissed her hungrily, and she allowed me.

When I had exhausted myself, she broke away from me and smiled. "Oh Will, you're such a little boy!"

"I haven't slept the last couple of nights agonizing over you." It was true, but I hadn't meant to admit it so openly.

"Meet me after work this evening," she said and skipped back into the pub via the back door.

We made languorous love that evening. I didn't want it to end. And I didn't want to face the morning when she might emerge as Medea or this new character Miss Julie, or someone else.

In between bouts of lovemaking, she introduced me to Miss Julie and her creator, August Strindberg. The young woman of higher class who is seduced by her manservant, Jean, on midsummer's eve, who is later spurned by him and goes mad; a fallen woman. Strindberg himself had been a victim of psychotic episodes during his life.

"It's intense, for I will be on stage for almost the entire play."

"Why are you playing these deep roles?"

"Hopefully, they will extend my range. They will also help me understand myself. There are pieces of Medea and Miss Julie in me."

"What happens tomorrow morning when we wake up?"

"You will go home tonight. I don't want a repetition."

"The subway would have stopped operating by now." It was three a.m.

"Take a cab." The resolute look on her face told me I had to comply.

I rolled out of her bed and started to dress.

"On the other hand . . ." her voice was cold, calculating, "if you can put up with me, you could stay."

The clothes flew off my body faster than they went on, and I was plunging back beneath the sheets while she laughed loudly and stuck my face between her legs. Oh, the joy! Let tomorrow go to hell!

And that's how we became steady dates. There was no "episode" the following day, but there were others, particularly when she was het up before a performance. I spent most nights with her for the next three months. She was also like a drug from my nightmares that had temporarily vanished.

The next blow-up was on the opening night of *Medea*.

"I can't fit into this outfit. I've got fat." She was trying to squeeze into the body-hugging, long dress in the green room. I had offered to help with costumes and makeup, as, with some students leaving early for the summer break, the backstage crew ranks had not panned out as originally envisaged.

I pulled in the two sides of the back of the skirt and managed to inch the zip up without pinching her flesh. "Don't make any grand gestures," I joked.

She waved her arms from side to side. "I can hardly move in this." The anguish showed in her makeup plastered face. A line of eyebrow paint had streaked down her cheek.

"Sit down in front of the mirror again," I said. "I'll touch up your face before you go on."

As I buffed her face again, removing the offending streaks and applying fresh paint, I could see the tears in her eyes. This was not good—histrionics were for the stage not the green room.

"Will, I'm scared." There was a tremor in her voice.

"You'll be fantastic once you get on stage. You will come into your own, and all of this will be forgotten."

Then she yelled at me, that vein in her neck protruding. "You don't get it, idiot! I've missed my period."

Before I could reply there was a knock on the door, and the stage manager poked his head in. "Five minutes."

As soon as he withdrew, Jacqueline cut off further discussion, "Leave me now. I need to compose myself and get into character." She was already looking into the mirror, practising various head movements. I could not have existed to her at that moment. Our recent conversation could never have happened.

I shrugged, deflated, and stepped out into the long corridor that led to the backstage area. I stood in the shadows behind one of the screen props in the wings and wished I could hide there for the rest of the evening. I could also watch the show from this vantage point without actually having to look directly into the faces of the actors, especially into her face.

She was spectacular that evening. Even though my view was limited, her movements and voice were at the right pitch and tone. The audience applause at the end of each scene was proof enough.

Then she did something unexpected during the finale, when Medea has ostensibly killed her children and is reporting it back to her cheating husband, Jason. Instead of turning to him stage-right, she swivelled around, back to him, facing where I stood in the wings and uttered her damning pronouncement. She was staring into the dark backstage where I lay concealed, and her eyes seared in my direction.

"I do not leave my children's bodies with thee; I take them with me that I may bury them in Hera's precinct. And for thee, who didst me all that evil, I prophesy an evil doom."

Then the curtain went up and the house burst into applause. I retreated to the green room to await her arrival and help her change.

When she did finally arrive, she tossed me two bouquets of flowers and grabbed a towel to wipe the perspiration from her face and under her collar.

"I told you, you would knock 'em dead," I said and didn't ask why she delivered those final lines at me.

After I had helped her out of her costume, hung it up and thrown a plastic wrap around it, I helped her wash the thick paint and foundation from her face. She then spent time straightening her hair, which had been bundled under the serpent head wig.

She grabbed my hand when she had finished. "Let's get out of here. I would like to skip the cast party."

I frowned. "But you worked so hard for it." I was looking forward to the party myself—and it was probably getting underway at the pub as we spoke—seeing as I was just getting to know these theatre types by volunteering for this gig. They were a lot more gregarious than us introverted writers with the weight of the world on our shoulders. "A few drinks would be good for you. For us."

"And what if I am pregnant? Do you want to damage your baby?"

I swallowed. "But...but we don't know that for sure yet, do we?"

"I'm normally regular with my periods, like clockwork."

"The stress of playing Medea could have caused it."

"If you are not coming, I'm going home on my own." And she was out the door with me trailing, carrying costumes, wigs, makeup bag, and used towels.

We never made it to that cast party. And over the weeks that followed the morning sickness took over, adding to the misery of her Bipolar moods. Her room got as messy as mine, although Tom tried valiantly to keep the common areas clean. Tom was not talking to me anymore, preferring to just nod when he left the apartment upon my entry. I felt responsible for her situation. I suggested she consider an abortion. That caused another row.

"Do you think I'm a quitter?" she yelled, dashing her plate down so hard that it broke in two, spilling pasta and tomato sauce over the dining table.

I held my ground for once, ignoring the spreading stain on the tablecloth. "You've got *Miss Julie* coming up in the fall. If you have the abortion now, you'll have a good two months to recover. Besides, you'll be back in shape for that play."

"No. I have to pay for my sins. I'm living my mother's legacy."

"Getting pregnant is not a sin. It is merely inconvenient at this time."

"Are you worried about childcare expenses?"

"It gives me the shivers. Yes. I haven't even sold my first novel yet. I guess I'll have to go out and get a job."

"It might give you a taste of the real world." She spat those words out. Before the pregnancy, when things got that heated, I would conveniently retreat to my own place until she had cooled down. But now I couldn't leave her in her delicate condition. So, I stayed and took the abuse, and her cruelty bonded us closer together. When the tension got too much, we had sex. Yes, we weren't making love anymore but rutting like animals so that the temporary euphoria and release would remove us from the looming crisis.

She moved into my apartment so I could look after her. She didn't seem to mind the mess for she had become messy. Tom was sad to see us go, or rather, her go but was also relieved to be freed from the responsibility of looking after his temperamental roomie. She stopped taking her uppers and downers, which was a side benefit and a great relief. But the mood swings got more pronounced, and I had to be on guard for the next flare up.

She didn't bother to go to the rehearsals in Stratford, for the baby bump was prominent by then. Instead, she wrote to Perrault explaining her delicate status and asking whether she could try out next year same time. Perrault sent flowers but made no offer for the following year.

"My acting career is in the toilet," she said and threw the flowers in the trash.

I got a part-time job in a supermarket loading grocery shelves and another one at the university library stacking books. I put my writing on hold—I was too distracted. In her fifth month, the pub asked Jacqueline to take a break and come back after she'd had her baby, if she was still interested. Mommies with tummies weren't Hooter's material.

"Misogynistic bastards!" was all she said before slumping into one of her dark moods.

We took lots of walks in the months leading up to her delivery. They were the most rewarding and revealing. We held hands, we kissed like teenagers out in the open. She was very fragile as the doors of opportunity were closing in around her. And we still had a lot of sex. Sometimes we fought when she was in a bad mood. Once, when she was on an even keel for a change, she stopped to pick up an abandoned doll in the park. She brushed the plastic hair and smoothed out the crumpled dress, cooing to it.

"Poor abandoned child. Like me." A tear ran down her cheek. "Now you know why I couldn't get rid of the baby. I was an abandoned child."

"But you had your mother."

"Who hated me every day for railroading her career."

And now this unwanted child is railroading yours. But I didn't say anything. I just looked towards the early setting sun over leafless trees. Soon I would be having to leave for my six p.m. shift at the supermarket, and I wanted to fill the unforgiving minutes with her.

"I don't know anything about you, Will," she said. "Is the baby going to have aunts, uncles and cousins on your side of the family? A grandma or grandpa?"

"I guess we should have sorted out those details before we created a baby. What does it matter now? Even if there are none of these relatives, I can't conjure them up in the next few months."

"Are you an orphan, then?"

"Foster homes. In one home, I had a pair of serial foster parents who did it for the money paid by the government. There were seven of us kids in that particular home, the only ones I would like to be related to. There were other homes too, but not as pleasant."

"Then there must be lots of aunts and uncles, and a grandma and grandpa. You must take me to meet them when the baby is born."

"Whoa! Who said they are alive?"

"You said there were seven kids in this one home alone, for God's sake! Someone must be alive."

She could see the pain in my face. I didn't want to revisit that particular story.

"You are looking at him," I said.

She dropped the doll. "Oh my God, Will! You don't mean—?"

"Highway accident while returning from a ball game. All died. I was the only one left at home with strep throat."

She threw her arms around me, and I needed comforting then. "Oh Will, you poor abandoned child."

A week later, a different conversation took place during our walk. She had woken that morning with a headache. Headaches with Jacqueline heralded mood swings, and I was very careful during those moments with the flippant remark that could be taken out of context and turned against me.

The weather had turned cold for November, and Jacqueline was having increasing back pains and needed to sit more often. We found a vacant park bench, and she rested while I picked up a stone and skimmed it over the pond in front of us, sending two Canada Geese squawking in opposite directions. I had been practicing this stone throwing more often in recent days, whenever we went out for our walks, as there hadn't been much else to do.

"Is this what you do every day, instead of finishing your novel?" Her voice was icier than the cold pond.

I turned back, shrugging. "Working two jobs doesn't exactly leave me with a lot of time to write these days. But I'll get back to it."

"You'll never get back to it. Distractions only multiply. You need to carve out a specific time and stick to it, no matter what."

I could feel her voice rising, and even though she was talking perfect sense, there was an edge, suggesting that I was not taking her seriously, that I was secretly laughing at her. I grabbed for a bone. "My agent is away in England until the end of the year. I have time to complete the final chapters before he returns."

"Rubbish. The baby is due in January. It's only going to get rougher from here. My back is killing me."

I walked up to her and started to rub her behind. It released tears in her. "I don't know why you bother so much. This baby isn't even yours."

I wrenched my hand off her back as if it was a hot coal. I jumped up and faced her, my reserve and guard fallen away. "What did you just say?"

She looked me defiantly in the eye. "It's Ross's."

"Perrault?"

"There's only one Ross I know."

"You slept with him?"

"How else does one get the leading role in *Miss Julie*?"

"But. . .you *didn't* get the part for getting knocked up." I wanted to smash her face into that pond and hold it below water.

"I miscalculated. My bad."

"How do you know it is his? We were both sleeping with you. And probably the rest of the cast of *Medea* too." I really wanted to hurt her now.

"A woman knows when that moment of conception happens. And it happened that one time with Ross, not in all the times with you, or anyone else."

The coolness with which she was making these statements baffled me. Was she trying to break up with me? In her seventh month of pregnancy, with no support mechanisms other than an absentee father hovering at e-mail distance?

"Maybe you can go back to Ross Perrault and ask him to look after this baby then."

"He has a family. Like my father had one when Mom got pregnant with me. You see, the cycle repeats."

"And you got me on false pretexts to support you in this charade?"

"I can leave now, Will. I know I don't deserve you."

"Where will you go?"

"Tom will take me back, if he hasn't sublet the space. And there are shelters for unwed mothers. I can't go down any further than I am now, Will. Oh, this headache. I hope it will go away now." She was holding the sides of her head and rocking from side to side as if trying to ward off some evil sound effect. Then the dam burst inside her, and she started sobbing, gyrating shudders that shrunk the rest of her frame over the bulging stomach.

Something gave inside me too. My anger dissipated. This woman was sick and very pregnant. In her misery she was trying to release me from the trap we were both in by saying these hurtful things. She was being considerate of me in her cold-blooded inconsiderateness. The baby was mine. It had to be. I went over and put my arms around her.

"Let's go home. A cup of hot chocolate will cheer you up."

She collapsed in my arms, sobbing. "Oh Will, what shall we do?"

The back pains kept getting stronger. The gynecologist we visited said that it was due to the baby pressing up against a nerve, a pretty common occurrence, not to be alarmed. But the pain continued. She wasn't sleeping at night, tossing and turning, getting up and pacing the small apartment.

One day, when I came in between jobs, I found her snoring in the middle of the afternoon. A bottle of pills lay on the side table. Prescribed by her doctor. I waited for her to wake, but she didn't, and I had to set out for my second job. When I came back from that shift at around midnight, she was still asleep. Nothing had been disturbed in the apartment, no plates used, no cans opened, the stove as clean as I had left it the previous night.

I lay down beside her and my exhaustion took over. When I awoke, it was the following morning, and she was sitting up in bed beaming.

"I had the most wonderful, pain-free sleep." She held up the bottle of pills. "A wonder medication."

"How long did you sleep?"

"Does it matter? I have recovered all the hours I lost in the last month. So, I'm even."

As the baby grew bigger inside her, the pain increased, and the more pills she took. In her eighth month, we stopped walking outside completely. Christmas Day was a drab affair. I brought home a plastic Christmas tree from the store and put some decorations on it. The library was closed for the holidays, so I had the time to do some baking, in addition to basting and grilling a turkey. Looking at her wrapped in a blanket on the sofa looking miserable, while snow fell outside, I felt a pang of nostalgia for Christmas in my foster home, the one celebration that was a fun one for us kids. My foster father, Percy, he of the seven foster-kid home, would be making the turkey and his wife, Maggie, would be putting the finishing touches to the pudding that was to be lit after dinner with the lights out; the brandy would encircle the dark blob of minced and baked fruit and blaze with a blue flame, and we would tuck in like hungry vagabonds, despite the mounds of turkey already devoured. Spoons would reach for the brandy butter, which would crown this dessert, the pièce de résistance of our Christmas meal. For those hours we forgot that we were nobody's children and our foster parents' house became our home. That's why I would claim Percy and Maggie's home as the one true home I had as a child, even though they were profiting from us.

And here I was in my own apartment with a woman who was bearing my baby—this was my family—like that other one in the manger, and yet I couldn't get that feeling of being at home. I was living with the uneasy feeling that this could all suddenly evaporate in front of my eyes. Jacqueline was so transient, a trace that would wash away like the aftertaste of a sumptuous meal, of even that memorable Christmas pudding.

I laid the finished turkey on the table that I had set for two. Jacket potatoes and beans bathed in butter; brussel sprouts completed the meal. I had bought a small Christmas pudding and a miniature of brandy for the "firing" later. As any other alcohol was out of the equation given how close she was to term, I had a jug of eggnog, sans rum, at hand.

"Happy Christmas, darling." I handed her a glass of the nog. She took one sniff and turned her head away.

"Oooh, that's awful. The smell makes me nauseous." I took her glass into the kitchen and didn't pour any for me either.

"Dinner is served," I announced, returning with a brave face.

"I can't eat. I'll puke."

This time I was deflated, and frankly, annoyed. If she didn't want to friggin' eat she should have told me before I went through the trouble of cooking. "Well, I'm hungry. Mind if I eat?"

She kept her face averted, looking outside the window. "Go right ahead." I could feel the resentment in her voice, but I continued to do as bidden. She rose and went into the bedroom.

I served myself a hearty plateful and sat down to eat. I poured myself a glass of rum to go with it. I had my back to the bedroom. The turkey was dry, but I hadn't made one in a long time, and when you've eaten that bird from one of its best cooks, my foster father Percy, it's tough to beat. Midway during the meal, I heard a muffled voice in the bedroom, perhaps Jacqueline was phoning a friend—good, that might distract her! I was slurping through the final crumbs and about to push my plate away when I heard the phone ring in the bedroom. It kept ringing unanswered. A sense of unease seized me, and I abandoned my soiled plate on the table and rushed into the bedroom.

She was lying on the bed, an arm thrown over her face to shield against the light. In the other hand she held an empty pill container. Her cell phone lay beside her; it had stopped ringing.

"I took them all," she said, matter-of-factly, stifling a yawn of dismissal. "Let me go but save the child. It's yours, not Ross's."

I was rooted to the floor, unable to move. One side of me was jubilant to hear her admit that the baby was mine. But the other side said that if she had lied the first time, was she lying now, just to get me to do her bidding? I was also petrified at what she had done to herself. What does one do for sleeping drug overdoses? Stomach pumps. But I didn't know what they were and how they were administered. I grabbed her cell phone and called 911.

The ambulance was late—Christmas Day, what did you expect?—and she began to convulse, a froth building up at the edges of her mouth. I tried putting my fingers in her mouth to get her to gag but she bit me and there was suddenly blood mixed with fizz spewing out of her. Her eyes had narrowed into a fixed stare, penetrating and frightening. I held her head down to drain the fluid oozing from her, but she kept resisting me, pushing me back with superhuman strength and lying back in the bed to choke and sputter. Just as I thought she would gag on her own effluence and die, the doorbell rang, and the experts rushed in.

I sat in the emergency waiting room of the hospital, chewing my nails. There was no one else in the room other than for a middle-aged woman with short greying hair, wearing a blue pantsuit with a briefcase beside her, poring over the contents of a manila file in her hand; she was thickset and short but had a matronly face. People don't get sick at Christmas, I reckoned, they must wait for Boxing Day to check into emergency rooms. But the businesslike woman with the briefcase was something else—who the heck works on Christmas Day?

Jacqueline had disappeared behind the grey double doors with the bars on them—a clear indicator that emergency room staff didn't want family members crowding their life-saving actions.

"They'll call you when she is stabilized." I swung around. The middle-aged woman was speaking to me. She had closed her file and was putting it back in the briefcase.

"You seem to have a lot of experience in these matters," I said.

"I have a lot of experience with Jacqueline."

"You *know*… Jacqueline?" I was staring at this woman. Where the heck had Jacqueline been hiding her?

"From the time she was a baby. Her father was in the background and her mother never wanted her. For awhile she was a ward of the state. I was her case worker until she was twenty-one. I still keep an eye on her. I'm Peggy Smithers. You must be William. Jacquie mentioned you to me."

"How did you know we were here?"

"Jacquie called me, soon after she had done her foul deed, as she called it." I recalled the cell phone beside Jacqueline in my apartment's bedroom. "She's done this sort of thing before. Once when she was nine, and once when she got pregnant at sixteen."

"Pregnant at sixteen? What happened?" I was reeling with all this new information. This woman was like a dark angel intensifying the colours on an already crimson palette.

"We gave up the baby for adoption. I am hoping we do not have to do this again. You plan to stick around, yes?"

"If she will not go around trying to off herself."

"That is never guaranteed. She has a…delicate temperament."

Just then those bolted doors opened from the inside and a doctor came out to give us the news that Jacqueline, and by extension the baby, were safe. Her stomach had been pumped of its deadly contents, successfully, and she was resting. We were to come back in the morning when she would be moved to a ward for observation prior to release.

"You'd better get some rest," Peggy said after the doctor had retreated behind those forbidding doors again. She picked up her briefcase and extended a calling card. "Call me if you need any help with Jacquie or the baby. Jacquie has become family to me now."

I wanted to detain this woman, find out about Jacquie's past, but she quickly walked towards the entrance doors and was gone before I could collect my thoughts.

Jacquie was released two days later, and I decided to stay home from work for the next two weeks or until the baby was born. My supervisors didn't take too kindly to my request, and I knew that they would get even with me sometime later, when I wasn't quite sunk so low. But I had to keep an eye on Jacquie; I didn't trust her anymore. We stopped having sex. I didn't want to hurt the baby I reasoned and was relieved when she agreed. Money was in short supply around our home, and I bought groceries with the last of my savings. I even stepped into the neighbourhood homeless shelter at dinner time, leaving what was in the fridge for Jacqueline. She remained in bed the whole time as any movement would increase the pain in her back. I made her soup, that was all she could handle. I moved the TV set into the bedroom, and we binged watched movies. Stealing glances at her, propped up on pillows, hair tousled, nightie soiled with traces of soup and biscuit crumbs, stomach swelling like a boulder in the middle of her body, I began to wonder how I could have been mesmerized by her. Under those sheets she looked like a discarded doll, morose, moody and mercurial. Now I only wanted Jacquie and the baby to be safe; physical desire for her had vanished.

My nightmares returned. I put it down to the tension I was under, the lack of sex, and the inability to write. I would jolt up in bed with the dregs of these nightmarish visions fading away; they were never courageous enough to stand their ground and reveal themselves to me in my awakened condition. But they lurked in the background to return and haunt me the moment I closed my eyes again. I was getting by on very little sleep during that time. And I didn't want to take sleeping pills myself in case I was passed out or groggy when Jacqueline got her labour pains. I was a walking zombie.

We never mentioned her sleeping pills incident. But something had happened to our relationship; a wall of decorum had dropped between us, and we both clung to it for protection. She seemed to be looking forward to having this baby, getting this suspended pregnant state over and done with. Two nights before the baby was born, she told me rather casually, "I've asked Peggy...you've met her, right?...to come and help during the days after the birth."

I felt sideswiped, but on reflection realized that I had no clue of how to help with babies. Besides, I had to return to work, or I would be out of a job, two jobs.

"That's fine. I'm glad we can lean on her." Then I decided to push it a bit. "How did you come to know Peggy?"

"She became my mother after my real one buggered off to California."

"She seems very attached to you."

She smiled distantly. "We have been through a lot of shit together. Peggy bailed me out when I got pregnant at a summer party."

It turned out, as she kept talking that all the kids at this party were drunk and Jacqueline had had sex with about four boys that night before she passed out. She didn't know who the child's father was. "They were all blond. Members of the senior hockey team."

"What happened to that baby?" I was pretending not to know much, but eager to learn everything about her past.

"Never saw it again after the birth. Peggy took care of everything. She put pressure on my father to get me into acting school afterwards for she knew that's where my passion was. Fat lot of good that did. Here I am, knocked up again." She spat the last words out.

"Well, our baby won't be given away." I sounded fake to myself, I'm not sure I was very convincing to anyone.

"Oh, yeah? Children cost their parents about a million dollars apiece to raise. We don't have a million dollars between us." With that she clicked on the remote to cycle up the next movie, putting closure to our conversation.

My agent wrote to me as he had promised early in the new year. The latest draft hadn't impressed him, he wanted one more from me before he would send it out to publishers. He had outlined the corrections I needed to make. I read through my manuscript and suddenly the novelty of it, of becoming a published author, wasn't there anymore. I was dealing with much more important flesh and blood matters now. I put his letter aside for later, whenever that was to be.

Babies do funny things to a new parent. Their arrival evaporates all previous conflicts and pre-occupations, bringing in new ones. They make you business-like and efficient, in order to function. They make you look at yourself intently and ask, "Was I ever like this?" They bring unexpected help from strangers. They bring divided families together. All of the above happened to us two days later when we both awoke in the middle of the night to drenched bed sheets.

"My water broke."

"I'll get a taxi." I'd have to pay the driver with a credit card for I had no cash.

"Call Peggy and ask her to meet us at the hospital."

We were quite businesslike. I liked that. My sleep deprivation had been pushed into another compartment, to be dealt with another day. No more moods, temper tantrums and sulks. We had a baby to deliver and we went about it with cool efficiency.

I remember holding the baby, born after a short labour: a boy, a scrawny, wrinkled and long creature, another blond (and my hair is brown, hers black) and asking that question, "Was I ever like this?" Then I remembered Ross Perrault's long blond locks and the bile rose in me. Peggy came dashing into the birthing room at that time and distracted me from further jealous thoughts.

Jacquie's maternal instinct flowed out as soon as her breasts started gushing milk, and we had peace for the next two weeks despite it being chock full of soiled Pampers, suckling breasts, squeals and more broken sleep. Peggy moved into our cramped apartment. I set up a camp bed for her in the bedroom, while the baby slept on the bed with his mother. I moved into the living room to sleep on the couch. I figured I wouldn't be having sex for a long time. No wonder marriages with children were so fragile and divorce rates were almost at fifty percent.

Lying awake that first night when everyone had returned home, I realized that our financial situation too was in chaos and couldn't continue. We needed money. I had to return to work as soon as possible. Then the kindness of strangers made its entrance: a cheque for $10,000 arrived in the mail the next day, from Jacqueline's father: "for expenses relating to the new arrival," it said cryptically. But I still went back to work because I felt that as the only man about the house, I had to provide.

Both supervisors took me back, albeit grudgingly. The supermarket guy actually said that they would not be booking any more time off for any employees until after the summer break, six months from now. He looked at me leeringly as he said that. I was glad to run to my jobs, leaving the women at home, returning only to cuddle with the baby for a few minutes before it latched onto one of Jacquie's breasts. I felt envious of this child who had ready access to those breasts that I, once upon a time, had full possession of. There was no intimacy anymore between Jacquie and me with Peggy and the baby around. Jacquie had cleaved fully to this infant, and it had become her sole occupation; I was like a ghost walking around the house, whenever I was around, and it wasn't only the lack of sleep but the lack of attention. Sometimes, in the way she unduly fussed over the baby, I wondered whether she was forcing herself to play the role of mother, one of her less rehearsed roles compared to Medea and Miss Julie, and one of her less desired.

I figured we had to give this child a name. Our resumption of fighting began from that discussion. Jacquie wanted to name him Ross (Ross?! Couldn't she have thought of any other name to quell the pangs of jealousy in me?) and I was vehemently opposed to that name. I retreated to the living room from the bedroom when Jacquie ended that discussion by throwing a feeding bottle at me.

We compromised eventually and the baby was named Roy. He was a good baby, and after the first two weeks of disruption, settled into a routine. Peggy was a balm on the choppy sea that was Jacquie. She sang to the baby, did the laundry, babysat, allowed Jacquie to take a walk in the park occasionally, and regaled Jacquie (and me, when I was around between jobs) with stories uncovered during her years as a case worker. Peggy had witnessed a lot of lives lived on the wilder side—hearing her made our lives bearable, made my orphan's life a shared one by many of this city's inhabitants. She also allowed me to sleep; if the baby woke at night, she took him out of his cradle and sang him gently back to slumber.

A month after Roy was born, as I was heading out to the supermarket for supplies one afternoon, Peggy said she wanted to buy some toiletries and asked to accompany me. When we were on the street, she came to the point.

"I think my work here is done. I must return to my home now."

I tried to come up with a counter, although deep down I knew she was right. "You have been a great help to Jacquie…and me. You are not in our way," I finally managed.

"I am. It's time you started stepping up to the plate. I'll visit from time to time to see how everything is going, but I need to give you space to grow as a family."

Peggy had another point. In this last little while, at least since the suicide attempt, Jacquie and I had drifted apart—that wall was getting thicker and higher by the day. I felt she had betrayed me with her selfish act of trying to commit suicide. And Jacquie was being wary of me. Whenever we were in each other's company, I could sense her eyes boring through me, studying my every gesture, her brain digesting my every word.

I nodded. "Very well. We'll miss you."

"You'll have to spend more time at home."

"I'm quitting the supermarket job. I'll hold onto the library one as it pays more, and the hours are better." I figured that Jacquie's daddy's ten grand would now have to be dipped into from time to time.

"I hope you are not put out financially."

"I'm sure Jacquie will remind her father that his grandson is starving if we run out of money again."

Peggy shrugged and got all businesslike for the rest of our walk. By the time we had returned from our shopping expedition she had given me all the pointers on bringing up a baby: how to change a nappy, how to check for a fever, how to make pablum to supplement breast milk, how to use a breast pump. My head was spinning.

As we entered our apartment building, she paused by the elevator as if something was troubling her. "You have to be mindful about the post partum period for a new mother. It will go a lot longer than the customary six weeks for Jacquie. Don't get into serious arguments during this stage. If it means sucking it up and eating humble pie, do it, for the sake of everyone."

I promised to be mindful.

"And make sure she attends her counselling sessions. Suicides try again and again until they finally succeed."

I nodded, recalling the Sylvia Plath story that I had read in my supplementary reading class. Hapless and gifted Sylvia, trying it several times until she got the art of suicide down pat and finally succeeded. I shuddered; the parallels were too close here.

Things were okay for the first two weeks after Peggy left. Jacquie and I focussed on Roy. That kept us from getting into any thorny existential discussions. But I noticed that when the baby was put to bed and we could finally relax from the day's activity, she would go into a shell, a sadness enveloping her face; she was like a passenger left stranded by a ship that had departed port. The look in her eyes was as if she was seeking a distant shore, knowing that she was never going to find it. In the morning she would be all business again, nursing Roy, piling up the laundry for me to do when I returned from my daily shift at the library, ironing the washed items, even cooking meals for the two of us when the baby napped. But at night, that sad face again. She only cheered up when Peggy would visit twice a week for a couple of hours; on those particular evenings she would watch TV after the baby was tucked in.

She went for her counselling sessions on Tuesday and Friday mornings, while I minded the baby. But as I was home with my hands tied, I couldn't monitor whether she actually made those classes. I once tried to ferret out information by asking the odd question, "So what did you cover today?" And she replied, "Old hat stuff. I went through it the last time too. They need to upgrade their program." I didn't ask again.

I found the role of "active" father a difficult one. I was an inept dad. My sleep deprivation was upsetting my concentration. I would invariably get the pablum composition wrong, and Jacquie would throw the mixture away as she wanted it just right to agree with the baby's delicate stomach. I left the odd stain on the feeding bottles after washing them, which also didn't cut the mustard, her mustard. And I had to get up when the baby cried at night as Jacquie needed her sleep in order to deal with him during the day when I was at work. I didn't have Peggy's hypnotic singing skills; I usually put Roy into a worse mood until his mother awoke and took him to her breast to calm him, giving me evil glares for screwing up yet again.

I staked my place back in the master bedroom soon after Peggy left. But Jacquie was still "out of bounds," she informed me coolly; her vagina was too battered after the birth, she claimed; she wasn't psychologically ready, she said, whatever that meant. Not wanting to risk an argument I accepted her position and relieved myself in the bathroom on that first night I moved back, more to assuage my disappointment and utter frustration than for salacious entertainment. It had been a couple of months since I had ejaculated, and I sat on the toilet seat after bursting my load, weak, limp but gloriously de-stressed and re-invigorated. Sleeping next to her every night after that, watching her swollen breasts and returning shapeliness, inhaling her womanly scent and imagining how it used to be was too much for me to remain quiet about. I started masturbating daily; it was like going to the gym for me, or a return to my adolescent days. You didn't think of the emptiness of the act but focussed on the singularity of purpose: stress relief from the suffocating prison that was my apartment where I had let all these "other souls" enter and take over. I got bolder in my acts of self-stimulation, even secreting a Playboy magazine into the bathroom for rapider results, which must have raised her suspicions. One day, as I stood inside the bathtub and was about to shoot my wad over the glossy magazine picture of a naked blonde with a 38-24-38 figure, Jacqueline walked in.

A bottle of shampoo, thrown with force rather than aim, hit me on the temple, making me drop the magazine from one hand and the hold on my throbbing member with the other. The next thing I remembered was the magazine being scooped up from the tub and ripped to shreds. Jacquie hadn't said a word during this explosion; she was methodically going about meting out her punishment on me. I had raised my hands instinctively after the shampoo bottle hit—a good thing too—for next came the basin in which some soiled baby garments were soaking in soapy water. As water splashed and flowed everywhere, floating magazine scraps away like flotsam, the shower curtain was ripped off its rings and flung at me. I slipped and hit my bum on the tap, sending a spasm up my spine, only to be met with the contents of the dirty clothes hamper emptied on my head as I slid down into the base of the bathtub. When I extricated myself from the smelly clothes, the door was closing, my attacker had departed, leaving me to wallow in my guilt and shame amidst the wreckage of the bathroom.

I slept on the couch that night. And the nightmares were worse, so I stayed awake for most of it. Towards dawn, instead of staring at the ceiling anymore, I went into the bathroom and shut the door and tried to restore whatever I could of its wrecked state as my act of penance. I felt like a downright heel.

When I apologized for my errant and disgusting behaviour it was Jacquie who broke into tears. "I'm not good for you anymore, Will, I'm a hopeless mother. This is not what I wanted to do with my life."

"It'll get better. Babies grow up. I'll grow up."

"Look at you. You need a magazine to jerk off to, and I can't fuck. The very thought of sex brings up the prospect of pregnancy and it's a turn off. You haven't worked on your novel in months. My acting career is toast. Don't you see? When you get off the treadmill of these careers that have such a short shelf life, you are never getting back on."

"I'll wear a condom from now on."

"You're not coming near me."

"I don't understand."

"No, YOU don't understand. You know who got me pregnant at sixteen?"

Oh, no. I was not ready for this revelation. "I thought it was the hockey player quartet at the summer party?"

"No, that was the official explanation to get away from naming a father."

"Oh. I see. Let me pick a name then. Lets see, my bet is, it was that dastardly Ross Perrault again, on a family outing with your dad and you. How's that?"

She laughed hysterically, swiping at her nose and eyes to rid them of tears and snot. "It was at a family vacation. Yes. And Ross was there, with his girlfriend at the time. But it was my own bloody father whodunit." She looked surprised too at what she had just said. It was as if a blanket had been ripped off her body leaving her naked in the cold outdoors.

"What! You were impregnated by your father?"

Now she looked triumphant at my discomfiture. I guess actors can turn on a dime when it comes to getting into and out of character. "I had just made contact with my father after all those years. The year Mom left for LA. He invited me on this fishing trip that he and Ross took every year to Algoma in northern Ontario. He wanted to get to know me better. I was mesmerized by my father. He was so handsome and manly. The cabin had two bedrooms; Ross and his girlfriend of the month shared one while Dad and I had the other. It was a proper pairing because I was his daughter and all."

"But that is incest! You were underage, so let's add pedophilia to the mix. Your father could be arrested."

"It wasn't all his fault. I seduced him."

I nearly choked. I had to pace back and forth in order not to fling something at her. Was there no end to the surprises coming from this woman? When I had calmed down, I said, "You're stringing me along, aren't you?"

"I'm not. It was the best role I played—the femme fatale." Her eyes were dry now, and she was looking at me coldly, her voice turning icy.

"Practice for your acting career that followed? Don't tell me that you were using these men as stepping-stones on your pathway to Hollywood or Broadway, or wherever the hell you wanted to get to?"

"I hadn't thought of it like that. It was pure and simple revenge. I hadn't known him very much before. He was just another slobbering middle-aged man, hungry for some pussy."

"But he was your father, damn it! Is there not an ounce of respect left in you?"

Her lip curled. "Dad told me that I reminded him of my mother as he made love to me. It was a magical moment when I got him on his knees and had him suck my toes—he's a fetishist."

"Stop it! I don't want to hear any more. You are saying all these hurtful and evil things to get even with me. I'm sorry I got caught shagging yesterday. I was jerking off because I wanted you desperately. Now can we stop? Please?" I was begging her.

"No, I won't stop. This shit has been corroding my mind for years."

"Is that why he sends you all that money. Are you blackmailing him?"

"He's paying for what he owes me. It's not blackmail—call it overdue child support."

That's when I forgot Peggy's warning and blurted out, just for my sanity, "God, you're screwed up!"

Then I walked out of the apartment. I couldn't understand a woman who could not fuck me for fear of pregnancy when she had fucked her father and got pregnant in the deal. Whose head was not screwed on right? Mine?

When I returned an hour later after walking in the park, punching the air several times, and regretting my outburst, there was a visitor in our apartment: Tom. He was holding Roy in his arms and cooing weakly. Tom looked like he had aged ten years in the five months since Jacquie had moved out of his apartment.

Jacquie looked manically excited. I immediately went on my guard. This was the high before another low. "Tom has brought Roy a musical chime. See." She pulled the contraption from inside the baby's cot and wound it, and it played "Twinkle, Twinkle Little Star."

I was grateful for Tom's appearance at that point, even though he didn't look in the greatest of shape. "Thanks for coming, Tom. It's nice to see you."

"Tom's got AIDS now—full blown AIDS," Jacquie said and burst into tears, convulsing on the floor.

I didn't know whose aid to go to: Jacquie's, Tom's, or the baby's who was wobbling in Tom's unsteady arms. Tom solved my dilemma by handing Roy to me and going down on the floor to Jacquie's assistance.

He smoothed her hair. "It's okay, my sweet. I didn't mean to bring you bad news today, but I guess it shows. I just wanted to see the baby before, things got a bit...er...difficult for me, travelling and that."

"I'm sorry to hear about your diagnosis," I offered.

Tom smiled, trying to shrug off his dilemma as if it was a pesky mosquito buzzing around him. "Been holding it off for years—Jacquie knows—and then it got me."

"Why do all the people I care for die?" Jacquie said, wiping her nose with the tissue Tom had given her.

"Well, I'm not dead yet. I could live for a long time."

"But you will die. Soon."

Tom laughed hollowly. "I have always admired your candour, Jacqueline. I guess that's why we were such good roomies."

"And you will get all those other illnesses that AIDS patients get—cancer and pneumonia and tuberculosis…and … and…" she was hysterical now, and I wanted this conversation to end. I wanted Tom gone.

Tom figured that too and rose. "Well, I didn't expect this to be such an explosive visit."

"Post-partum blues and AIDS are a bad cocktail," I said and took Roy into the bedroom to change his diaper. I heard them commiserating with each other, alternatively sobbing and comforting each other. My concentration was so shot that I had changed Roy's diaper three times over before pulling myself up and into the present.

I heard Tom finally taking his leave and the front door slamming. I had managed to put Roy to sleep after my repeated attempts with his diaper change. Then I must have dozed too, beside him, out of sheer exhaustion. No sooner had I dropped off than I was shooting up on my feet from the worst nightmare I had had in recent times. Roy had been in it—I recalled as I hung onto the fast receding dregs of that dream—and so had Jacqueline, but the details were foggy as usual. Getting my bearings—I was not only on my feet, I was standing up against the bedroom wall—I looked back towards the bed. Roy was awake and crying—no wonder, with his hysterical father sleeping beside him. How the hell had I got up and walked over to the wall without realizing it? Was I also sleepwalking now?

Jacqueline ran into the room, picked up the baby, and ran out again. It was an eerie image. I remained standing against the wall, frozen, watching them, as if I was watching a movie, or living inside one of my nightmares. Was I still half asleep, or had I just seen what I had seen? Given my sleep-deprived state I was not sure anymore.

I shrugged and went into the kitchenette and fixed myself a coffee, black. Coffee always brought me down to earth. I took the steaming mug with me into the bathroom to drink, shave, shower and get ready for my afternoon shift at the library.

When I emerged from the bathroom, Jacqueline was in the living room, cradling the baby in her arms and looking outside the window towards the park where I had been working out my frustrations earlier.

"Sorry about my nightmares. Are you going to be all right today?" I asked. "This hasn't actually been a good day."

"I'll phone Peggy." She had her arms wound tight around her body, and I could see she was trembling. She must have laid Roy down somewhere. This scene was getting so disjointed, I was having difficulty with its continuity. I went over and hugged her from behind. Her shuddering shook me too. She swung around and clung to me.

"Oh, Will. I'm so scared."

"I'll call in sick today. I want to stay with you and Roy." I knew this was not what I should be doing with a supervisor who was looking for any excuse to fire me.

"No, you go to work. I'll call Peggy."

Reluctantly, I left for work.

But I couldn't concentrate at work. At four o'clock I took my break and called the apartment from a payphone. No answer. I called Peggy, no answer; I left a voice message on her answering machine. I was not supposed to get off duty until the library closed at eight thirty p.m. and tried to put off the impending sense of disaster from my mind. At six p.m. my supervisor came to me, scowling, "There's a call for you. You can take it there." He motioned over to the phone on the checkout counter.

It was Peggy. She sounded breathless. "I was out the whole day with my sorority—a trip to Casa Loma. Got your message. Have you heard from Jacquie?"

"No. She was supposed to call you."

"She hasn't. Will, this is not like her. I'm going over right now. Can you get away?"

I looked around me, the supervisor had returned to his office on the third floor. "I'm coming," I said.

Asking one of my colleagues to cover for me, yet knowing that this was going to probably get me fired, and dreading what I was going to face when I got home, I hightailed it. I ran, as I didn't have the money for a cab, and I couldn't trust the wait for the streetcar. It was about ten traffic intersections to the apartment, and I got there in a lather despite the February cold. I was also sharply alert for a change when I arrived.

There was a crowd of people outside my building, with a police car, fire truck and an ambulance flashing their multi-coloured lights. An old man was walking towards me, shaking his head.

"What happened?" I asked, knowing the answer even before he spoke.

"Accident," he said, still shaking his head, in disgust, I thought. "Woman fell from one of the top floors. Jumped, says an eye-witness." He walked away muttering, "What is this frikkin' world coming to?"

I dashed through the throng but got to the ambulance only as the loaded gurney was being pushed inside and the doors being closed. Turning on my heel, I ran into the building and up the eight floors of stairs to our apartment. When I burst in, I heard Roy crying in the bedroom. His nappy was wet, and he had drooled and puked all over his shirt and bib. Tom's gift, the musical chime, had fallen on the floor and its winding key had become dislodged and was lying a few feet away—had Roy flung it? With his snarling, blood-engorged face, this baby did not look a happy camper.

Just then Peggy rushed in. I must have left the front door open.

"Oh, Will—"

She looked aghast. I didn't give her time to collect her breath but thrust Roy into her hands and checked out the rest of the apartment. A cold draft was blowing into the living room—the sliding door to the balcony was cracked open. I shut it without even wanting to go outside. The answer I was looking for was on the dining room table, written in her artsy, cursive scrawl, a style I thought was going extinct.

Dear Will and Peggy,

I have to call it quits. I don't know what is reality from acting any more, one blurs into the other. I can't make out the lies I tell people to hurt them from the lies I tell myself in order to get through the day. They say this act of lying makes us good actors or writers, but since I am neither, I am cursed. Please look after Roy. I am sure, between the two of you, you will do a better job than I can. Will, you and I cannot raise this child—we are not good together. Don't hold yourselves responsible for what happened to me. This was of my doing.

Jacquie.

I broke down because in her last act, she had not blamed anyone else but herself. I realized then that despite all her flaws she had loved me.

That's how I came to leave Toronto for Ottawa. In that act of handing Roy over to Peggy, I was also handing him over to her to do with him what she had done with Jacquie's first baby. She could give him up for adoption, raise him, or dispose of him as she saw fit. I felt a sense of relief when passing that blond-haired infant over to her for the last time—how could he be mine, after all? Blond hair? Humans are capable of rationalizing anything, I guess. If what she had told me was true, Jacquie had condoned incest, and here was I rationalizing abandonment. I had promised Jacquie not to give the baby away, but I was doing it without remorse now that she wasn't around. But I was suddenly relieved of a great burden, two burdens in fact, in one shot. Make that three in one, for the next day, my supervisor at the library fired me. It was easy to take that train ride to Ottawa and start life fresh—no baggage, only memories that were buried in Toronto, and only to be regurgitated by the snow falling in this park today in Ottawa, as I was on my way to meet another woman who reminded me so much of Jacqueline.

Chapter 4

"Can't you see? She's you. A dead ringer." It had taken three beers to get through my Jacqueline story, and at that point I wasn't paying much attention to my choice of words. When I had last unburdened, to the guru at the retreat, I had stopped short at the Jacqueline story and of recounting my orphaned childhood, but this time it had all come flooding out.

The Hog's Head pub was unusually crowded due to the snowfall outside, filled with workers snagging a pint and waiting for the blizzard to ease. The weather for me was a roaring torrent of emotions that I was trying to medicate with alcohol.

"Well, I'm not pregnant, and I'm not an actress, and I'm not twenty-two anymore," said Dee, staring at the single glass of chardonnay she had been nursing all evening as she listened to my story.

"And now that abandoned child, Roy, is after me. He's tracked me down from some ministry database. Perhaps he works at the ministry. Maybe he sits in the office next door." Suddenly going back to Darlington's poky office beside the ByWard Market was anathema.

"As a father, if you were his father, you didn't damage him as badly as we were treated by our fathers, Jacqueline and me," Dee said.

"But I abandoned him. Your fathers came back into your lives, kept in touch, paid for things. I just escaped."

"But you provided for his adoption."

"Peggy did. I just handed the kid over to her and said sayonara."

"You were in shock. Jacqueline had died by suicide."

"After I knocked her up and ruined her career."

Dee was starting to get irritated by my self-incriminations. I was too. I ordered a fourth beer. This was going to be my last one for the evening.

Afterwards, snow or blizzard, I was going home with Dee and burying my sorrows, and my cock, inside her for comfort. I needed comfort. I excused myself and went to take a leak.

The washroom smelled of high-grade urine, a snowfall will do that for you. Men pissing at will—that was new, as I had been in this pub several times before and the three urinals were rarely all used at the same time. I wondered for a moment whether I was in a movie theatre, or in a movie itself. As I was adding my frothy piss to the deluge already excreted by the other patrons, the hair on the nape of my neck started to rise. I felt I was being watched, from behind, by one of the guys lined up to take a leak. I couldn't swing around less I spray everyone behind me and get arrested as a flasher. So, I continued to pee, feeling trapped, hoping my generous stream would cease quickly, so I could turn around and catch my spy.

When I finally ended, shook the dregs of micturate off, tucked the big fellow back in my pants and swung around, there were only two guys standing in line: an old geezer with a beer barrel stomach who gratefully grabbed my vacated spot and farted as he dropped his pants, and a young, punk-haired guy (his hair was half blue and half red) in tight pants and stud earrings. The punk was staring into his phone as if taking a selfie. As I moved over to the sink to wash my hands, the punk turned abruptly and left. My suspicion was immediately aroused. This two-tone-haired guy had been photographing me, not himself. I abandoned drying my hands halfway and ran out after him, but he must have ducked out of a side door for he was gone by the time I re-entered the pub's main lounge.

When I returned to our table, Dee had a whimsical look on her face as she stared out the window at the thinning snowfall. She took my hand and looked at me playfully.

"You know, you too are now living your second chance. The guru was right." The significance of her words, in light of my washroom encounter, was to hit me later, much later.

I had to grudgingly agree with her. I didn't tell her about what had just transpired in the washroom. Well it wasn't really anything, more a flipping of my mind. I guess my nerves were getting ahead of me. Perhaps that punk was just a…a punk…Perhaps he had got tired of waiting to take a leak and stepped out into the alley to shoot against the wall. Given the snowfall, he probably would have more privacy in the alley than inside that smelly washroom. Instead, I stared at my drink. "What do I do now? Give up my cushy government job because of this guy following me?"

Dee slapped my hand playfully. "No, of course not. You ferret him out. Let him make the first move."

"What happens if he follows me and pushes me in front of a moving vehicle? He knows what I look like." I doubted that punk had the strength to push me, he looked so…girly.

"Or she. This could be a fake moniker being adopted by a woman who has taken a like, or dislike, to you. Perhaps a jaded fan of one of your books." Her face was alight with impish humour.

I drained half of my glass. "Well, you asked me for my story and now you know."

"But you haven't told me about being raised in a foster home. Or homes. What was it like? Did you ever know your biological parents?" She was leaning forward, insistent. But I was not going there. Not there.

"You know that kind of information was kept from us orphans, although now you can go hunting for it. It's too painful for me to even try. Do you want me to do the same thing that this Roy fella, if he is indeed Roy, has done?"

"Well, you should be able to find out something. It may give your life an anchor. You are unanchored, if you take my opinion."

"That's why I write, I guess. I pass along like a ship, observing, recording, never anchoring."

"I'd like to help you get anchored."

I took her hand gratefully. "That'd be 'a consummation devoutly to be wish'd.' I've been seeking that all my life."

She took another sip of her wine and pushed the glass away. "I suggest you finish that beer and we go back to my place. The snow is easing. A nice warm bath and bed will work well for you tonight."

"Ah, another 'consummation devoutly to be wish'd,'" I said, guzzling the rest of my beer, farting, burping, and grabbing my coat. "And some sex, perhaps?"

"We'll see, greedy boy."

Darlington called an emergency meeting the next day. A curt e-mail commanded us to convene in his office at two p.m. It was urgent, was all it said. I dragged myself to this meeting. The previous night with Dee had been so marvelous that getting out of bed was actually painful.

When I entered his poky office there were about half a dozen people already assembled including Darlington and his assistant Maddie who was handing out sheets of paper to those gathered. I thought this was supposed to be a cyber unit committed to no more felling of trees—not so in Darlington's antiquated world, it appeared.

Darlington nodded at me and looked at his watch. "Grab a seat anywhere." Seating was at a premium. People were seated on desks, tables, or standing. The guy standing next to me, holding a Starbucks paper cup, smelled of curry; he wore a tee-shirt and jeans. Next to him, a fat Chinese guy in a baseball cap, seated with legs propped up on Maddie's desk, was lost staring into his smart phone. Two other South Asian looking young women were seated in the only available chairs and poring through the contents of the papers being distributed.

"Hi, I'm Rakesh," the curry-smelling guy said, extending a limp hand to me. "Me and Chung here are the IT guys." He nodded over at the Chinese guy wrapped up in his smart phone who didn't even look up.

Darlington clapped his hands standing in the centre of the room. In these close confines, everyone's odors were mixing in with the curry smell closest to me: deodorant, perfume, coffee, sweat.

"Thank you all for coming at such short notice. I'll get right down to it as I know you have busy schedules. We have received an alert that a foreign government run cyber crime ring is trying to infiltrate government owned servers with a view to influencing the upcoming election, like they did in the States in their last election. As you know, the environment is a top priority these days, global warming has finally been proven real while our provincial leaders continue to stick their heads in the sand pretending it isn't so."

Rakesh had his hand up and interrupted Darlington. "Is it the Russians?"

Chung looked up from his smartphone for the first time. "No, it's the Chinese, man." He returned to his phone.

Darlington cleared his throat. "Well, let's not go making blanket accusations here. Suffice to say it's a foreign entity that does not mean us well."

"They'll never break into our servers," Chung said, staring into his smart phone. Chung obviously felt this meeting was a waste of his time and that it was taking him away from his computer game or whatever he was involved in on his smart phone.

"Thank you, Chung," Darlington said. "And Chung is right. We are not worried about an internal hack, so to speak, but an external disinformation campaign on social media. That is why I want you folks to be vigilant and alert us to any trending hashtags or news articles that tend to undermine our PR efforts on the environment."

One of the South Asian women replied, her head swaying to and from, her voice lilting as if in song, "Fatima and I have been checking Twitter and Facebook. So far nothing has come up."

Rakesh whispered in my ear. "We call them Tharuni the Twit and Fatima the Face. They each specialize on one of the two platforms; you can guess which from which."

"Thank you, Tharuni. Yes, I know your vigilance is thorough. But we only need to let our guard down slightly, and an abhorrent post can go viral. Stay vigilant."

I hesitated over bringing up the issue of predators like my tweeter. Was that out of context to this meeting? Then pre-empting me, Rakesh piped up. "What about people assuming our identities and putting up fake posts?"

"Or people attacking us for posting what we do?" Chung said. This time he kept his head raised waiting for a reply.

"Well…er," Darlington seemed to be casting into the ether for the answer, "well, then you should bring that to my attention as soon as possible. We will notify those platforms to have these miscreants blocked or cancelled."

"I complained once, and they blocked *me*, not the fake guy," Rakesh said.

"Well, if you bring it to *my* attention, an official letter from the department should be sufficient to clarify who is who to any social media platform," Darlington said.

I decided that I was not going to tell Darlington anything about my mysterious tweeter until I knew more about his (or her, as Dee had said) identity.

Fatima was waving one of the sheets of paper that had been distributed. "Are these all the sources of misinformation we have caught so far?"

"They are," Darlington replied. "These accounts have already been blocked with the social media companies. But others will crop up."

"As machine learning improves, even the grammar will get better very shortly," Chung said. "Makes it harder to identify."

"Yes, especially as the reading public reads less and learns to write in hashtags," Darlington said drily. For a moment I saw the disdain of the academic in him, someone who had been reared in a classical atmosphere and was now unhappily transplanted into this world of bits and bytes and curry smelling brown people, the only ones who could be hired cheaply and who worked hard. He turned towards me. "What say you, Smallwood? You're a writer."

I decided to be vague. "Writing for the web is certainly different from writing a novel, I've discovered."

"But far more effective, no?" Rakesh said. "Gets to the point, yar? I could never figure out that book called *Ulysses* that we were supposed to study in university. The characters were not even in Greece, they were in Ireland, masturbating in public—pardon my language, ladies." But Fatima and Tharuni weren't even paying attention. They were scanning the handouts and commenting to one another. Maddie had a wide grin on her face. Sometimes I wondered whether Maddie was a robot.

Wanting to move the subject away from literature, I said to Darlington, "Perhaps if you could give us some indication of this foreign social media threat, we could prepare our defences better."

"All I know, or have been told," Darlington paused as he carefully framed his words, "is that no two attacks are the same, no two sentence structures are the same. They either have an army of writers, or a very clever algorithm. Rumour has it that the recent spike in opposition to the carbon tax was catalysed by these posts."

"That was just our provincial politicians," Chung said.

"But they got these ideas from popular trends in social media. The bad guys start these trends and our dumb politicians—*provincial* politicians, if I may qualify—latch on to them."

I figured I'd better make a contribution to this meeting and asked, "Am I to take it that I should continue to make my posts on a status quo basis, despite this threat? Although every action may have an equal and opposite reaction?"

"Yes, Smallwood. I have not been advised to curtail our PR campaign. But watch out for those equal and opposite reactions. We need to control the message here."

The meeting broke up with us being no more wiser than that there was a threat out in the cyber waves. I figured that Darlington and other staffers had been advised by their bosses to communicate this threat to their underlings, and he was just going through the motions.

Exiting the meeting I asked Rakesh if he would have a coffee with me as I wanted to pick his brains on an idea. His buddy Chung muttered something about being late for a server upgrade operation and rushed off, his security pass blowing in the wind off its lanyard.

"Ah, I like Starbucks only," Rakesh said, eyes alight. I figured Starbucks equalled "more information," and Tim Hortons equalled "no information." So, we walked into the Indigo store at the other end of the market and headed upstairs to the Starbucks counter.

Over a Café Americano that cost me a small fortune, I told Rakesh about my dilemma with the tweeter.

"Check his tweets and retweets. Check his followers and his hashtags—that will tell you the type of character he is. Follow him on Twitter and see if he follows you back."

All good advice that I decided to take as soon I got back to my laptop.

"Send him a message on Twitter too. Threaten him. See if he backs off. And check others who follow you, because he may decide to drop off and re-join you under a new account name. Usually, all his followers of his old account will also be his followers on the new account as that is the easier way to keep a following. Also, make another account for yourself, follow him, tweet adoringly about him, flatter him, and after a suitable time make an appointment to meet him."

"You're kidding!"

"Why not? Many people are coupling by meeting online."

That Café Americano was well worth my investment.

When I returned to my apartment I launched straight into the Hunt for the Mad Tweeter. I followed Rakesh's advice. @abandonedchild97 tweeted only on environmental issues, mostly angry protests about western governments and their lack of concern for third world countries, about waste dumping, plastic in the oceans, fish caught with toxins in them, yadda yadda. This guy was on every environmental lobby site you could find. I rested easy—okay, so he was a paid tweeter of the Environmental Lobby who spent his time doing what, in a sense, I was doing, except that I was a paid voice of a G7 government. The moniker @abandonedchild97 didn't say much about any kind of environmental activist either. Perhaps he had adopted this name before he had been hired. He didn't have more than a couple hundred followers, and the only accounts he was following were a few well known lecturers and consultants on the environment, a holistic health centre, and people who looked anarchic and anti-social; many in this latter group also looked gender queer with spiked hair, earrings, heavy make-up, Mohawk haircuts and torn away clothing. When I followed some this dude's tweet feeds, his followers came across as a bunch of nihilists, fed up with the existing world order but with no practical alternatives to offer. Reject, reject, reject seemed to be their mantra.

One particular link, a recent one, caught my attention. It did not jive with the environmental ones.

It read https://secretlifeofalternativesex.com. I clicked on it, and it took me to a home page of a concrete wall with the word "Enter" scribbled on it in charcoal. I clicked and out popped a password screen. It needed numbers, special characters, letters and a total length of not less than ten digits. Damn! I was about to retreat in defeat, then thought, on a whim, why not use *@abandonedchild97* as it conformed to all the password requirements. I typed that password in and voila, I was in! I was soon to regret it.

The concrete wall motif dissolved into pictures of naked women and men; men with men, women with women, and men with women. I am not a prude when it comes to appreciating the beauty of the human form, but these people seemed to be in an ecstasy of pain: bared lips, bloody mouths, drool, and sperm dripping from all orifices. The bodies floated in a mist with some techno music playing in the background. A menu showed up with items such as "sado," "machismo," "beasto," "homo," "lesbo," "kiddo," and I kind of knew where this was going. To confirm my suspicions, I clicked on the first menu item. A pop up on the corner illuminated to say that I had a credit of $54.23 and would I like to continue? I answered in the affirmative and the pop up dissolved into a counter on the side of the screen, counting down the seconds of viewing time that I, or my predecessor (i.e. @abandonedchild97), had purchased. My eyes were drawn to the act of violent sex on the screen. A man in a masked hood was going at it with a naked young man. The camera swivelled around 360 degrees and there was no doubt where the hooded guy's massive cock was embedded. When the camera came around full circle, I could see the pain on the young man's face. Then I nearly jumped out of my skin. The young man's hair was two-tone—half blue and half red—and when he stopped snarling in pain (or was it faked pleasure?) for a moment, I recognized the youth who had been taking photographs in the pub's toilet.

Was I dreaming? I looked closely again to see if I was superimposing images from my own consciousness onto the screen, but no, there he was, the same guy. Quivering with revulsion, I shut down my browser. I staggered over to the window and opened it, letting in frigid air. I didn't care about catching a chill. I needed to breathe; the room had become stifling.

It took me a few minutes to shed those images and return to my laptop. There was no doubt, this was one heck of a high-class porn site for A-class weirdos. And rich ones too, for when I had switched off, barely five minutes into my viewing experience, my credit had shrunk to $45.35. If this young man in the video was indeed @abandonedchild97, why would he want to see repeated pictures of himself being abused by a hooded man? It would more likely be the hooded man wanting to see his conquest repeatedly, I reasoned.

And did the number 97, the last two digits of this moniker, stand for 1997? The year I handed Roy in for adoption. You can see why I was spooked by this guy. I trolled through his tweets going back almost a year. Midway, I came across a period where he had been only sending inspirational messages out with hashtags to LGBTQ groups. It sort of fit with a red and blue haired guy. I guess I was stereotyping, but I was on the hunt here and stereotypes helped. But his more recent tweets and hashtags had become darker, including that porn site joining his list of favourites. I decided to send him a threatening note. I checked out the holistic health centre. It was in Ottawa, on the other side of town from me. Maybe it was his place of employment. I would pay it a visit tomorrow. Overall, the picture of @abandonedchild97 that was emerging was of an angry young man, abused or abusive, intelligent in his observations (far smarter than his waco band of followers), incisive in his criticisms, and sympathetic to the marginalized.

I ended up deciding *not* to send him a threatening message per Rakesh's advice, in case I spooked him and lost him altogether.

My research had been so consuming that I hadn't noticed the hours creep away. It was six p.m. by the time I extracted myself from the various hashtag alleys and tweet volleys that following @abandonedchild97 had taken me down. I wondered whether Dee would tolerate a second consecutive night of sex. We were supposed to be on a weekly schedule now, remember? But given my fragile state yesterday, I wondered whether I could prevail against her strict rationing.

I called. I got voicemail. I left a message. By eight p.m. she still hadn't called. I was not spending an evening alone. I was going to take myself down to a restaurant and have a taxpayer funded meal for a change.

Chapter 5

I headed along Somerset into the heart of Little Italy. It was reassuring looking into the windows of family run restaurants: couples sitting at intimate tables covered in checker cloth, poised in romantic gestures, steaming platters before them, the proverbial bottle of wine sticking out like a totem while waiters provided the only movement inside these intimate nooks, romantic hideaways in this staid, bureaucratic city. I missed Dee.

Then I saw her, not Dee, but Susan. She was sitting at a window table I was passing. Her young accountant sat opposite her and was raising a glass of red wine. I stopped some distance away on the sidewalk, not wanting to attract attention as a peeping Tom. But they had eyes only for each other, and she was raising a water glass in response to his toast. She was fuller in face and beaming. I could never recall her beaming with such abandon in all the time we had been together. I had also never seen her with such a full stomach during our relationship. It was obvious, from the angle I was observing her, that she was very pregnant, at least eight months along, which would mean she hadn't wasted much time after we split, may have even been getting it on with her accountant during our last days together. I felt kicked. I couldn't bear to see such happiness, a happiness that I had denied her. I turned on my heel and walked away fast. Damn, the guru's philosophy of the circular nature of things!

I walked toward the river and turned west on Albert Street and cut south back into Little Italy but far away from Susan's dining place. I kept walking to dispel the image of my second wife and her guy and regain my appetite. Maybe pasta and seafood would be the right comfort food tonight, a substitute for sex. Guzzled down with a litre of Chianti. I swung into Alberto's, a restaurant I had visited once after I had recently moved to Ottawa. That was in the time when my books were selling, and I had money, and my agent had big plans for me. But nothing had panned out, and I had retreated from places like Alberto's and settled for Tim Horton's.

The place had been renovated and expanded and a full bar ran across one end. Mature uniformed waiters were in full swing, balancing trays of food and sweating, but projecting a veneer of professional calm towards their guests; the place was crowded. All the higher end places were usually crowded in this city that never endured a recession except when there was a parliamentary budget cut. And they were especially packed when Parliament was in session and MPs from across the land were in town with their entourages and hangers on. I caught the eye of a waiter sporting the dignified name badge of Caruso and asked whether I could have a table.

"For one, signore?" He wrinkled his nose. His "one" sounded like "Whaan." This guy must have just got off the boat from Italy after serving as a waiter for thirty plus years in his home country. And he must live with his Italian/Canadian extended immigrant family in Little Italy so that he would never have to venture out of his ghetto for anything. He looked cocky and self-assured in his self-contained world. I was stereotyping again.

"Yes. Is that a problem?"

"The bar, signore. Only the bar." He handed me a menu and sauntered off.

I scanned the menu. There were many combinations of pasta and seafood. My mouth watered and my belly rumbled. So I pushed my way up to the bar and grabbed a stool between two groups of suited men who were drinking and talking loudly, gesticulating with hands that were bound to slap me on both sides.

Ah well, it's good to get out occasionally and experience life, I figured, even though sometimes the results are unexpected.

My waiter, Caruso, had come around the bar. "A drink-a for you?" I had to hand it to him, he was an expert at covering his patrons.

I ordered a glass of Merlot.

"And to eat-ah?" He looked around him and shrugged. "Better order now-ah. Si?"

"Pasta with lots of seafood," I said, pushing the closed menu back at him.

"Ah, The Seafood Arrabiata or the Pasta Pescatorre?"

"Surprise me, Caruso," I said and dismissed him. He flashed his hands in the air and left with a "I fixa you a-good."

I sipped my Merlot and remembered the last time I had been here. My third novel had just been published and my agent, Sam Muller, had treated me to dinner. He had been full of plans for translation rights and even a movie deal. The world had been my oyster on that night. How quickly the bottom falls out. I had managed two more novels, writing to the formula of that third breakout novel, but the spark hadn't caught. The winds of popular taste had shifted, and I was left chasing after a whiff of fame that had wafted past my nostrils like the elusive smell of garlic inside Alberto's.

The glass of Merlot vanished, and I signalled Caruso for a whole bottle of the same vintage. What the heck!

He opened it with flourish, flashed the cork under my nose to show me how pristine and undestroyed it was, and then decanted the bottle for me in a flagon that he put down on the bar. This made me nervous for the gesticulating patrons on either side of me were positioned to knock it for a home run in no time.

Caruso noticed my consternation. "Ah! I keep it a-for you, below here. You can reach-a?" He placed it below the bar on the working counter used by the bar staff. I imagined liberal doses of margarita, soda, scotch and beer flying off the hurried hands of the bartenders and spilling into my flagon, so I downed my glass and filled it one more time before giving it up to the mercies of the bar staff on that perilous lower counter. Now if I lost it, at least it was half consumed.

Two glasses of wine in rapid succession was a bit much, even for me, and I began to feel tipsy while nursing my third. But it was a good antidote to having seen Susan. And for not having Dee with me. Turning nonchalantly to the guy on my right who had his back to me and was waving dangerously with his outstretched hand, I said, "Mind my drink, buddy. It's a bit crowded in here."

The guy turned around with an annoyed look on his face, and I was staring at Professor Darlington.

We both jerked out an embarrassed "Hi." Darlington tried to shield the guy he was talking to with his bulk, but in his jerky movement I caught a glimpse of a large, wrestler-type with a smashed nose and shaved head in a suit bursting at the seams. The man looked like he had recently returned from a Caribbean vacation for his face was deeply sun tanned.

"Are you a regular here?" Darlington shouted above the din.

"No. I came here to celebrate my employed status."

"We pay you well, do we?" Darlington smiled, and his anxious face started to relax.

"The government does. Introduce me to your friend. It's lonely in here despite the crowd." I was getting kind of bold—blame it on that third glass of wine.

"Oh. Yes. Meet Igor. Igor, this is Smallwood, a colleague." Darlington motioned his hand half-heartedly between his companion and me and coughed.

The wrestler looked annoyed at being introduced but extended a beefy hand and crushed mine. His eyes were cold steel and dead. When I painfully extricated my numbed hand, Darlington said, "Well, we were just leaving. Nice to have bumped into you." He turned to Igor and arched his head towards the doorway.

Igor tossed back his drink, fished some notes out of his jacket, tossed them on the counter, and nodded. "Let we go." His voice was a cross between a bass and a baritone. They filed out, Darlington meekly following his hulking companion.

I turned back to my wine and pulled the concealed flagon back onto the counter and poured my fourth glass. I stared into its crimson depths. Darlington and a Russian, what did that mean? And a Russian Darlington didn't particularly want me to meet. And only this morning we had been discussing foreign interventions. Fishy.

And talking of fish, Caruso arrived with a steaming dish. "My speciale, for you, signore." The calamari and shrimp entwined in the fettuccine, exuding vapours of garlic, herbs and lemon, got my tongue all twisted, and I didn't stop to ask whether this was the Arrabiata or the Pescatore—I just dived right in.

I was wiping off the sauce with my garlic bread after having walloped that entire meal—we had been taught never to waste a drop of food in my foster homes—when the very act took me back to the image that had haunted me so often. I had not been visited by it for a long time now, but moments like this, when I was indulging in something that I didn't find myself deserving of or entitled to, this fancy meal in this gourmet restaurant and the wine to dull my guard, were bound to trigger it, I guess. Or maybe it had been the sight of Susan.

There I am with my suitcase. The taxi has dropped us off and the case worker is ringing the doorbell. The door opens and this portly man in a waistcoat stands in the threshold and ushers us in. The inside of the house is untidy. There is a male child in diapers crawling on the floor and there is something spilled on it. An assortment of toys, many of them broken, litter the vast room, empty of regular furniture.

"Come into the playroom. The other children are at school," says the portly man. He is surveying me from head to foot. A woman appears at the doorway. She is wearing a soiled apron and her red hair is tied up in a bun; when she smiles her teeth are stained, cigarettes. The house doesn't smell of cigarettes, though. Palmolive liquid—that is the smell in the house, and something else from that spilled liquid beside the little boy.

"Sign these papers," the case worker says and extends his hand. The man signs eagerly, the woman shrugs and mutters, "Another mouth to feed," and waits for the man to finish before adding her autograph.

The case worker smiles. "But you are getting paid for it."

"Not enough!" the woman barks and signs the paper, almost tearing it in the act, then flings it back at the case worker.

The door closes behind him. It was as if the light is going out for me as that door closes. I am surrounded by the smell of Palmolive, and vomit—that is the second smell—the boy's vomit.

"Sorry to rush off there." A voice beside me.

I came out of my daydream. I was still at the bar. My plate was empty, the platter licked clean, as they say. And my glass of wine rested next to the flagon that had one final glassful in it. The voice was beside me. I glanced up and for the second time that night was surprised by the sight of Professor Darlington.

"Oh, I thought you had gone for the evening," I said.

Caruso appeared to take away my plate, and as he did so, Darlington expanded on his speech with his hands to say, "Igor was anxious to get back to his hotel. He has a flight tomorrow," and hit my flagon sending my last glass of wine to splash on our veteran waiter's white uniform.

"Mama Mia!" screamed Caruso.

"Blast!" yelled Darlington.

"Damn!" said I.

"I'm dreadfully sorry, my good man," Darlington apologized to Caruso, pulling out a twenty-dollar bill from his jacket pocket. "Here, get that uniform dry-cleaned." Caruso was dabbing at his jacket, oblivious to the offer. He soaked his napkin at the tap behind the bar and kept rubbing away as if he had been scalded from an overturned caldron.

"It's gonna cost him more than twenty bucks," I said, throwing another twenty on the counter. I had begun to like Caruso despite his obnoxiousness.

"Oh, my God. And I've spilled your drink too." Darlington looked like he was regretting coming back. "Let me buy you another. And one for me."

When Caruso had reasonably composed himself and was looking like a wounded soldier after a bloody battle, we ordered another glass of wine for me and a double scotch and soda for Darlington. Caruso fulfilled our order, demanded we pay right then and there, and left. I never saw him for the rest of the evening.

"Are you enjoying your job?" Darlington asked.

"It's the steadiest one I've had."

"Don't let the bureaucracy kill you."

"Why? Has it gotten to you?"

"You don't have to deal with the higher ups. I do. Stuffy civil servants who have never had to worry about a paycheque. Life is an entitlement to them."

"Like academia, isn't it? You should be comfortable in that world."

"That's why they hired me. But it doesn't mean that I like it."

"What would you rather have done?"

"Always wanted to be a writer."

I burst out laughing. "You're kidding."

"Then I met you and realized that I was not missing anything."

I looked across at him to see whether he was trying to goad me, but he was gazing into his glass, a distant look on his face. "Well, actually, the writing was secondary. It was more to clarify my philosophy of life. What I really wanted to do was to own a resort down in the Caribbean."

"Really?" *And spy on all your half naked guests with your binoculars, you pervert!*

"Bought a piece of land in Jamaica once. Cleared it and opened a B&B. Hurricane wiped it out. Then I found out the guy I bought the insurance from had done a flit. There was no insurance."

"Are you going to try again, now that you are older and wiser."

"I am older and wiser and widowed."

"Ah, sorry to hear that."

"Wife had an insurance policy though. Helped me buy a place here five years ago. Lakeside property. But it's not the same as the sunny Caribbean."

We drank in silence. I was in awe that he was opening up to me so much. Perhaps he'd had too much to drink this evening.

"Another round?"

"Sure." What the heck, if he was prepared to talk, I was prepared to listen.

During the next round he told me that he had no children although he had "endured" a long, unhappy marriage. "Work was a distraction from an empty and unsatisfying nest. I was relieved when she passed."

"Work killed my second marriage too," I offered. Susan was coming back to haunt me.

"Women. We need them, and then we have difficulty managing them. My wife preferred to eat and eat. And I preferred to stay away from her binging. Diabetes got her in the end."

"Yes, just like my second marriage. To a tee. Without the diabetes, though. We didn't have children, either."

Darlington squinted at my last comment, then seemed to let it pass.

"Now all I have to dream about is taking another punt at that island in the sun. Yes, to answer your earlier question, I'm going to have another go at it, now that I only live to satisfy my own desires and pleasures— something I should have embraced years ago, before plunging into the role of the stable family man laid down for me by my settler forefathers."

I thought I'd change the subject. "That Igor fellow doesn't look like a guy you'd want to hang out with."

Darlington dropped his voice. "Official business. I was asked to take him out and entertain him. One of the not so pleasant duties entrusted to me."

"Is he working on the environment in his country?"

"I'm not at liberty to say. Actually, the less you mention him the better, got it? It's complicated. Sometimes we are forced to mix with unsavoury characters in order to cover our backs."

"Is that why you came back? To remind me?" I thought I'd get that one out of the way. Clear the air.

"Let's have another round," he said, ignoring the question. We never mentioned Igor again.

We had several rounds. I was in topping form. Susan had been cast back into the slagheap of history. Here I was getting a man I had never taken a liking to—although now with his unburdening, I felt I could smell the human in him—my boss, to buy me drinks.

He was definitely a well-read man. We talked about history, and I told him about my historical fiction work, specializing in the French Revolution and the Reign of Terror that followed and in Victorian England, both gold mines of intrigue, romance and violence, and fertile grounds for entertaining fiction. He understood and was well versed in the eighteenth and nineteenth centuries, launching into his own impressions of Napoleon, Robespierre, and Queen Victoria and of their strategies for usurping and consolidating power.

"Keep everyone unsettled, especially those close to you. Robespierre was the master."

"And Napoleon?"

"Surprise attack. His forte. Also, his downfall when the Russians surprised him on his long march."

"What about Victoria?"

"Get people to clothe table legs for their lewd symbolism while enjoying the most ribald carnality herself."

"No one is interested in those anti-heroes anymore. Their values don't make sense in the twenty-first century. My book sales proved it."

"Fiction is a fickle mistress. What readers fail to understand is that a historical fiction book is a time machine that takes them to a period when values were not what they are today. They need to buy into that deal. But they judge the past by the present."

"I read your expose on the guru. Were you judging the present by the past? I'm not sure you made a dent in him, though. He's still operating in Toronto."

"No, I wasn't bringing the past into it. That we are anachronisms is a given. But I haven't finished with that guy. However, I have other bigger things to fry at the moment. This misinformation campaign, for one."

"The guru might argue that you were running a misinformation campaign against him and his cohort."

Darlington went red. He knocked down his drink. "You know, my boy, one day you will come a cropper in government service by being too outspoken. I like your candor, but you must learn when to zip it at times."

"Let me buy you the next round to make amends for my loose mouth," I said and signalled to the barman. "Although, the more I drink the more I gaff."

We staggered out of Caruso's close to midnight. We had got comfortable by then at trading barbs and laurels with each other, for both had begun to blur by then. We stood outside letting the cold air sober us, waiting for a taxi to take him home.

When the taxi arrived, I heard him give an address in Nepean.

He leaned through the window and said in parting, "You are a lucky devil, Smallwood. Sleep well between the divine lady's thighs tonight." The envy in his face oozed from every pore, making me shudder. Then he settled back in his seat and waved as the taxi sped off.

A man lost, I thought, an anachronism, as he admitted. A man from another time whose values did not work today, just like my books. A man who hates being in the skin he is in. Who seeks the escape of hedonism. Who desires that which he cannot have. Did he have to *manage* his wife? He destroyed his marriage through neglect, like me. And the heavens rewarded him by destroying his island haven in a storm. Was that the genesis of his anger that made him smash his camera—a vivid image that still unnerved me—as if he were God raining down a hurricane on an island in the sun? A complex man, indeed. And a dangerous one.

As I walked home, I wondered about the daydream that had played out on that bar counter. This was the first time whole images and sequences had appeared, faces of people I could freeze in my mind. My prior dreams had been flitting ones, like strobe lighting, fade-ins and fade-outs, sufficient only to frighten but never to recall afterwards. Had I tapped into some submerged reservoir of memories this time, and was I now able to dredge out the dirt of the past? Had the meditation sessions I'd had with the guru, but which I had never really practiced since, started to give my goblins faces and perhaps names? Had Darlington's presence at that bar been the catalyst?

Chapter 6

Hey Cunt—read the newspaper headline today. Your PM is a liar. I have ammunition that will blow his story to pieces.—@abandonedchild97.

The message was awaiting me when I logged in the next day. I didn't get the newspaper anymore—who did?—I just bummed into online sites to gather what I needed. I scanned CNN, CBC, and the free sections of the Star and Globe but didn't find anything that had quotes by the PM—the free sections had news that were days old anyway. So, I hauled myself down to the convenience store and picked up the current copy of the Globe. There it was, on the front page:

Prime Minister to make Environment his main re-election platform.

Now that he had conquered trade in his last term, the PM was turning his attention to the environment and climate change in a big way. Smart, given his southern counterpart had departed back to coal, and tough-man right wing leaders around the world were burying their heads in the sand about the warming planet; Canada would seize the lead in climate change initiatives. The article went on to say that, given his tough stand on pipelines, the PM was looking to cease all activity in that area and fund clean air initiatives instead. There was also a picture of him standing next to an electric car model, the production of which was going to be in Canada in a conventional auto plant that had been closed a couple of years ago and had now re-opened as a re-tooled autonomous car production facility.

All good things. So, what was my mad tweeter so het up about?

I asked him via tweet message.

Oh, wait until I leak his emails with the Yankees on his pipeline plans, came the reply.

What the heck was our PM doing with the Americans trying to build new pipelines when he was going about shutting them down? Fake news?

Fake news, I suggested.

Fuck you, came the instant reply. *Just watch me*. Who was this guy? Another Wikileaks?

He was even using the elder Trudeau's famous words. Would a twenty-something even know who Pierre Elliot Trudeau was, let alone the crucial epigrams that engrave his prime ministerial gravestone?

I wondered whether it was time now to reveal this crank to higher authorities. To Darlington for starters. However, I decided not to. Not yet. There was one more lead I needed to pursue.

The cab dropped me off at the address on a side street that had skipped the development boom of the city. Pre-WWII bungalows, wooden, rickety, small, and painted in multi-colours, ringed both sides of the narrow street. High-rises were going up behind this street. Number fourteen was needing a fresh coat of paint, the red on its wooden walls was peeling badly. The deck that ran across the front creaked as I stepped on it. The sign across its threshold said Holistic Meditation Centre. I rang the doorbell.

When the door finally opened, the man in dhoti and sweater, with a purple turban was none other than Guru Swaminanda.

I jumped back in surprise as the guru smiled, raising an eyebrow.

"Come in, come in," he said. "I've been expecting you."

"Expecting me? What the heck are *you* doing here? I thought you operated in Toronto?"

"I have a branch here. Many politicians have issues and are in need of meditation. Besides, after Professor Darlington wrote that glittering article about me, business has fallen off in Toronto."

As he was still bowing and extending the hand of welcome, I stepped into the house. The air smelled of josticks and stale curry. He led me into a living room that was bare except for mats and cushions arranged in a circle in the middle. He gestured for me to have a seat on one of the cushions. I remained standing.

"Some *lassi* for you?" He went out into another room, and I heard the rattle of cutlery.

"No thanks. I am in a bit of a hurry. I want some information about someone associated with your organization."

The guru returned, and he was holding a glass containing a frothy yellow liquid. He sat on a cushion facing me and drank deeply, exhaling with eyes closed.

"Ah, it is always refreshing and opens the senses, this *lassi*. How is Divine Secrets? Are you still together?"

"Very much so."

"Yes, I could see there was a spark between you two. Give her my regards."

"I will. But as I was saying—"

"Yes, you were saying. . ." The guru had opened his eyes to drill me with those piercing ebony orbs.

"Do you know a guy who goes by the Twitter handle of @abandonedchild97?"

The guru frowned and shook his head. "I don't use social media much, other than to post our events. I find it is very distracting. Many politicians who come to see me suffer from the twin maladies of what I call the Twitter Twitch and Facebook Fatigue."

"How about a guy who has half red hair, half blue. A thin young man of about twenty?"

"Oh, you mean Roy?" The guru was studying my reaction.

My skin started to crawl, and I struggled to retain my composure. I had not expected it to be so easy.

"Does he live here?"

"He drops in from time to time. When he is in need of a place to stay and some comfort for his tired soul."

"Is he homeless?"

"More or less."

"A derelict? A juvenile delinquent?" *Thanks to me.*

The guru sighed. "You people have so many labels for those who are living a harder life path of their own choosing. Has it ever occurred to you that they may be stronger than us who have easier lives?"

"How can I meet him?"

"I can tell him you called when he next visits. Leave your card."

And have him run for the hills!

"No, that would not work. Can you tell me where else he hangs out? I can check out those places myself. There is some urgency—"

"I don't know exactly where he hangs out. He 'hangs out' in dark places, and I don't frequent them. Clubs, mainly. Every time he returns, he looks the worse for wear. Either having engaged in a fight or fleeing from some messy relationship. I taught him to meditate. He meditates with us, heals, and goes out again only to return shortly thereafter. He has been doing this on and off with us for about five years."

"Is he on drugs?"

"He was selling them once. To survive. The last time he showed up, he was serving in a restaurant."

"Where?"

"At the ByWard Market, but I don't know at which one."

I gave the guru my writer's card. "If you are able to convince him to contact me, give him this card."

The guru fingered the card. "If I may ask, who is he to you?"

My son?

"A relative."

"Why the urgency now?"

"There is some money he has inherited. I would like to give it to him." We both knew I was lying, but that was beside the point.

"And you didn't even know his name until now," The guru sighed. "Certainly an abandoned child, Mr. Smallwood, isn't he?"

"Let's say that it would be in his interest to meet with me."

"That would indeed be good for him at this time in his life. He needs a friend. Please do not do him any harm, for he is too fragile. I will keep your card and give it to him if he shows up. He was last here three months ago, so he is due for another drop-in shortly."

As I took my leave from the guru, I paused on the doorstep. "Guru Swaminanda, why is it that almost everyone I met at your yoga retreat is coming back to me in a different form and under different circumstances? At this rate, I only have to bump into Phil and Marge Davis to complete the circle."

"Life is circulatory. What goes upstream, eventually flows downstream. That is why I knew I would meet you again. As for the Davises, it's unlikely that you will meet them together now. They separated last month, after their children finished their degrees. It appeared that the children were the only tie holding them together."

"Oh, brother! Another bloody statistic. Another middle-aged couple discovers their true selves!"

"They come to see me, independently now. Both are still trying to find themselves even though they initially believed that separation was the answer."

"Well, give them my best wishes—independently. Given that we all seem to be one big happy family, crashing into each other all the time, I guess I am bound to meet them sometime."

When I left the ashram, I was convinced that the guru knew more about Roy and me than he was letting on.

I went to the ByWard market and trolled the restaurants. It was lunchtime and the market area was busy, restaurants full to overflowing. I stood in each line-up by the entrance, "waiting to be seated," and scanned the interior of each respective restaurant, looking for a flash of red and blue hair and leaving before I was seated if I saw no evidence of Roy. I got lucky at the fourth establishment. Roy was moving between tables, holding up a tray with glasses in one hand and a water jug in the other. Not even a server, a bus boy!

I stood in line to be seated, and that took thirty minutes. I didn't take my eyes off the boy. And he was so busy that he didn't notice me standing behind other patrons anxious for a table. When I was finally seated—an inconvenient to find table that had kept me waiting for half an hour—I composed myself for my first visitor, the bus boy. When he came over and filled my glass with water, standing over my shoulder, there was no sign of recognition other than for the tremor in his hands, which could be put down to the weight of the full jug, or fear. Before he finished pouring, I turned around and said, "Hello, Roy. Or should I say @abandonedchild97?"

He jumped back, spilling water on the floor, and stared at me, his face a mix of emotions ranging from discovery to anger. Then he said, "What do you want? I rent my body out only at night, not in the afternoons."

Now it was my turn to blush. "I wasn't meaning to 'hire' you," I managed. "Why have you been sending me those threatening tweet messages?"

"I don't have a clue what you are talking about."

"Aren't you @abandonedchild97?"

"No. I abandoned my twitter account a year ago when people started sending me death threats. Men. They fuck you, and then they want to kill you."

The server was making her way over to my table, cutting off further conversation. She was even suggesting to Roy with her eyes that he should cease further engagement with a prospective big tipper. Perhaps Roy was limited to serving water because he was known for his caustic tongue with patrons. I managed to slip him my card, which he took quickly, secreting it away like a conjurer. Then he moved to the next table, and I was left looking at the beaming server who wanted to take my order.

During my meal, I caught glimpses of Roy working the far end of the room. After awhile, he stopped appearing. When I was paying my bill, I asked my server whether the water boy, Roy, was still around.

"Oh, he had to cut short his shift. Migraine attack."

As I was at the ByWard market, I decided to call in at the office. Walking over, I pondered on the bits of information from Roy. "...renting my body at night...men...they fuck you, and then they want to kill you..." He was a male prostitute. He frequented dark places like clubs—per the guru—where men picked up whores. He had picked up the wrong type of client a year ago who was now trying to kill him. Was that assessment right?

When I got to the office, only Maddie was around. I decided this was as good a time to snoop as any on the other matters that were playing on my mind.

"Hi Maddie, how's it going?" I said breezily, pulling up a visitor's chair, indicating I was here to stay awhile.

She was dressed in a black polo blouse that covered the lines and pouches on her neck. A layered white pearl necklace added the finishing touches of camouflage. Her hair was blonde, but it was too perfect, so I imagined there was a regular dying involved and the most recent one had been in the last twenty-four hours. Late fifties, I had pegged her at, trying to look younger.

"This is an unusual visit?" There was an expectation in her birdlike eyes. She had literally no chin, but her voice sounded ebullient today. Was it because she had me to herself without her boss in the vicinity?

"I was reading an article in the newspaper today about the PM's new election platform and wondered whether you could dig out some position papers that I can write my next set of blog posts from."

Her eyes drifted back to her computer, a bit disappointed, I thought. "I'll see what I can come up with." Her voice had returned to its familiar monotonous, business-like tone, the one she employed when Darlington was around.

As she went searching through databases, muttering to herself, I spread my hands on her desk and leaned over. "How long have you been working here, Maddie?"

That quick look of interest again, as she peered up from the computer. Her lips pursed coquettishly.

"It's been a life sentence. Straight out of college."

"Well, you must have a solid pension to look forward to. I have none of that kind of security."

"It's not as secure as it appears on the outside. Most people get some terrible illness after they are persuaded to retire and go out to pasture. And by the time we get out, it is too late to start a second career. Unlike you."

"My second career—this one—is the best I've had so far. It finally pays the bills."

"But you must have had some adventures in your life of being a writer."

"Misadventures, more likely."

She laughed and her face flushed.

"Ever been married, Maddie?"

She flushed even deeper. "I wish."

"I wish I hadn't. See? The grass is always greener..."

"You probably never met the right woman."

"That is for sure."

I saw the look of interest in her eyes flame up. The fleeting and tempting thought. The older woman syndrome. I was at least a dozen years younger than her. Would it work, she seemed to be wondering out aloud as her eyes betrayed her thoughts. Then she looked back into her computer screen and resumed her businesslike voice, the thought of romance being pushed into the background where it would remain safe. At her stage in life, matters of the heart must be dangerous.

"There are a couple of conferences the PM attended recently where he talked about the environment. Let me e-mail you the links to his speeches."

"Have you worked for Darlington before?" I pressed, believing I had an inside edge.

"A few times. Whenever he has been on assignment to us." Then she leaned forward, looked around, and lowered her voice. "He has a problem with his hands."

I imagined a younger Maddie with a horny Darlington pinching her rather flat bottom, or better, staring at her bust like he had done with Dee.

"He was widowed five years ago," I offered in our boss's defence.

"This hand problem was way before he lost his wife. We speculated around the office that he had doctored her insulin when she slumped into that final coma. He kept that poor woman on a leash all her life."

I let her words sink in. Over at Alberto's the other night, I had actually felt sorry for the widower, Darlington. Now I wasn't so sure. I recalled him mentioning his wife's life insurance policy. How convenient!

"There are workplace harassment rules. Why didn't you go to an ombudsperson or something?"

"I wouldn't be looking forward to my 'fat' pension if I had done that, now would I? To his credit, he has been keeping his hands quiet lately, though." She chuckled.

Because he likes younger women, and you are past it. But I didn't say anything to burst her bubble.

I returned to the apartment and began writing an article about the new election platform. As promised, Maddie's e-mail links had arrived, and they provided me enough grist for my piece. Given the sensitivity around this political platform, my article was bound to need higher-up approval. I was going to have to show it to Darlington and get his written consent to post it. I drafted and re-drafted the piece many times and decided to let it sit overnight. I always let the controversial pieces sit and marinade. I was just putting my laptop away when my cell phone rang.

"It's Roy," a breathless voice said. "Can we meet at four o'clock at the Museum of Civilization?"

"Sure," I was equally breathless, not wanting to let go of him this time.

It was a bugger of a place to get to, in Hull, so I took a cab. I could suddenly see why he wanted to be here. Only tourists came here, the locals went elsewhere. If he wanted anonymity, this was as good a place as any.

I saw him standing in the main hall of the lower level under the giant totems. He was wearing the black shirt and pants of his water boy uniform from earlier that afternoon.

"Coffee?" I suggested. "It's good for migraine."

"Don't be a smartass. That was just an excuse. But you can buy me one in the cafeteria."

We went into the cafeteria, bought coffee that cost a fortune, and sat at a corner table out of earshot of even the tourists.

I decided to open with the most pressing thing on my mind. "You said someone was after you."

"Sometimes you can't please everyone. Do the things they want you to do. Sometimes you find out things about them in bed that they wouldn't want you to find out."

"Like what?"

"Are you a cop?"

"No."

He studied me carefully before replying. "Sometimes men in prominent places, politicians, have secret desires they don't want their constituents to know. It loses them votes. I am a secret desire. Especially if the man portrays himself as a strong heterosexual."

"So, they mate and kill their secret sexual partner afterwards?"

"Yes. Like the preying mantis."

"Someone has gotten a hold of your old twitter handle and is using it for other purposes. Can you not cancel it?"

"Not after this length of time. He has probably changed passwords. Now I would be considered the fake one."

"Can you not go to the police with this guy's identity and have them put a restraining order on him?"

"I have no proof. We always met one on one—no witnesses. Besides, he is not the person who will do the killing. They pay underlings to do their dirty work. Restraining orders don't work."

"Well, your two-tone hairstyle is not exactly a good cover. If you pardon my observation it cries out like a billboard. That's how I spotted you."

"I was a skinhead when I met him. I thought this hairstyle would be different. In fact, I passed him on the street once a few weeks ago, and he didn't notice me. Gave me the creeps, though."

He wasn't obviously going to disclose names, perhaps he didn't know, so I didn't say anything more about his mystery lover that would spook him. Even though I had him in my clutches, I could lose him just as easily. At these close quarters, his resemblance to Jacqueline was stunning. He didn't look like me at all.

He spared me by switching the conversation. He still hadn't touched his coffee. "Who are you?"

I was taken aback by the question. Then I realized that if he wasn't the one sending me those threatening tweets, he wouldn't know me. I also remembered him taking a selfie behind me in the pub washroom. What was that about?

"Why were you taking pictures inside the Hog's Head washroom?"

"Because I work there—one of my many part-time jobs—and I was trying to protest to the management how unclean the washrooms get when there is overcrowding. How else do you provide them proof unless you take pictures?"

Fair enough. A blank again. I tried another tack. "I knew your mother."

"Which one? I've had several. Foster ones."

"The one who gave birth to you. Jacqueline."

His hostile look dissolved and tears squeezed at the edge of his eyes. "My birth certificate said 'Parents Unknown'."

"They had to do that to make you eligible for adoption. Do you remember anyone who could have been family when you were growing up?"

"There was a woman called Peggy who came to see me from time to time whenever I changed foster homes. She had permission to take me for outings, and she took me to church with her lot and taught me to pray. She stopped coming when I was eight. Later, they told me she had died of cancer. I started going bad after that. Even God had let me down. Peggy was the only link to a family I ever had."

My palms started to sweat. My hunch with this kid had paid off. Peggy's name was the clincher.

Now it was my time to tear up. His story hadn't been any different from mine as a child. If the next generation is supposed to be better off than the previous one, then that hadn't happened here.

He was looking at me, realization suddenly dawning. "Are you my biological father?"

"I could be. I wanted to be. But there was some doubt."

Then it poured out of me again. The Jacquie and Will love story. The whole sordid affair. I sat there in that cafeteria and let it all hang out. When I finished, darkness was falling over Ottawa-Hull, and the museum was closing for the day.

I was shaky on my feet, the emotional outpouring had sapped me, and he took me by the elbow as we joined the crowds exiting the building.

I offered to give him a ride in my cab, but he said that he lived just a few blocks away and would walk. I think he was embarrassed to show me where he lived. We stood at the entrance of the closed museum, both reluctant to part company. Taxis passed us looking for a hire, each driver leaning over to glean our intent, and then drive away or pick up another, more interested, fare. I figured I was going to be walking over the bridge back into Ottawa.

"We should get tested," he said.

"For what? I don't carry any diseases on me. At least, none that I know of."

"No, I didn't mean that kind of test, though I've done many of those, too. I meant genetic testing."

He was making sense. He seemed to have ascended into a position of strength during my collapse into self-pity.

"That sounds like a plan." Any excuse to keep me connected to him for the moment.

"I know a place that does it for cheap. I took one of them when I checked out my gender."

"Why did you have to do one of those?"

"Because I am gender fluid. When I have enough money saved, I want to explore transitioning."

I had to hold on to him in case I fell. This was too much information all at once.

He smiled. "Why do you think men find me attractive?"

"You had all the right male parts when you were a baby, if I recall."

"But not in my soul. You obviously didn't look into my soul when I was a baby."

I nodded, humbled by his observation.

"Let me make an appointment with the clinic and call you," he said.

"What happens if we are not related? Could we still remain in contact? Guru Swaminanda said you needed a friend. I would like to be your friend."

His jaw tightened. "You'd better pray that we are not related. I would take a long time to forgive you if you are my real father."

I let that sink in. The enormity of my crime of twenty years ago sank in, and delivered by its victim, it was more powerful. I couldn't do more than shrug and accept his verdict. "Fair enough. I will accept your decision. But I would like to stay in your life, either way. I was also an orphan. And I never knew my parents. At least, in your generation there is more information available."

"Which also confuses and compounds the situation. 'The grass ain't greener. . .' as you say."

I gave him a hug in parting, and he melted into my arms. I could see why he was attractive to men. I held him out at arm's length and surveyed him again before letting him go. "I'd like to help you stay safe. From those predators who are after you. If you will let me."

He smiled. The weak smile of a child this time, not that of the angry young man when we first met. "Thanks. But I know how to look after myself. Now I must go. I start my shift at the Hog's Head in an hour, and I need to get home and change."

I watched him go, melting into the fog that had crept up the river.

Chapter 7

"Well, you've certainly been busy without me," Dee said after I finished recounting the events of the last couple of days. She had repented for ditching me on the night I went to Alberto's and had shown up at my apartment after my meeting with Roy. We made love, desperately for me, accommodatingly for her, and while lying in bed, I had started talking.

"But he is in danger, and I have to save him."

She laughed. "After all these years? He seems to have managed well on his own. Are you instead trying to save yourself from your orphan childhood? You haven't yet told me about it."

"I told you. It is too painful. I seem to have blocked most of it out. I get occasional snapshots of it, memories that flash and disappear. They get triggered during happier moments and in times of stress, sometimes when I take a drink and let my guard down. As if some bad angel thinks I am not deserving of any happiness."

"Aren't you happy with me?"

"I am."

"Have you had any of those memories when you are with me?"

I sat up in bed. "You know, you are right. I haven't. Not yet, anyway."

"I'm a safe harbour, eh? A sure shot?"

I took her hand. "You are the most stable person I have met."

"I thought Susan was."

"She was. But I wasn't at the time. She was the transitional woman for me. I thought I was going to be the famous author surrounded by fawning women. Now I don't have any of those illusions. You could say I have become stable and dull."

"Did you cheat on Susan?"

I frowned. She was digging deep again. "Let's say that I did a lot of author tours back then. There were many hotel rooms in lonely towns. I signed books after readings, often in public and sometimes in private. I realized how Ross Perrault must have felt when he made his appearances in various venues and invited star-struck women into his private suite afterwards."

She smiled. "Poor William Smallwood, the once-famous writer."

"My next career will be as a blogger. No author tours, no fawning fans, but a steady income. I'm even developing some ideas for a private blog funded by advertising after this government gig is over."

"I thought you were writing a new type of novel. Given up so fast?"

"Oh, I write down bits and pieces of what happens daily. A kind of Proustian recording of events. At first, I thought there would be something to it. But my life isn't that interesting. I now realize that my Proustian prattling will not amount to much."

"You could write the story of Roy. Make it into a political thriller. I see a title "The Dark Secrets of My Member of Parliament."

"Oh no, don't start me off into another popular genre. From historical fiction to political suspense. It will be like asking a car mechanic to repair a ship."

She rose from the bed, and I admired her naked silhouette against the window. She pulled my dressing gown over her bare body. "There is some news I have to give you."

Oh, oh. Here comes that bad angel again!

"Good or bad?"

"Depends on how you view it." She paced the bedroom. "My client wants me in Toronto for the next couple of months. They want me to finish the work onsite as they are opening their new corporate headquarters in April and everything must be ship shape before then. I will be working with the architects and interior designers on getting the right colour blends, different art pieces to match the decor of each meeting room and boardroom and so on. So, it needs to be a focussed, team type activity. None of this remote work will cut it."

Before I could open my mouth to protest, she went on, "And they have commissioned six more pieces from me for their corporate training centre on the eighteenth floor, as they like what they have seen so far."

I opened and closed my mouth several times, and all I could utter was, "Where will you stay?"

"A room at the Royal Excelsior with a daily allowance, on company account."

"Can I visit?"

She chuckled. "I'll have to ask permission. But I'm sure we can work something out."

I was happy for her. Ever since her return from the retreat, her new career direction had been taking off in a series of progressive waves, while mine was bopping up and down like a toy bucket in a swimming pool.

She came back to the bed and took my hand. She kissed me deeply and I tasted the love, felt it envelop me. "I'm sorry to leave you by yourself at this stage in Ottawa, darling. Especially with your paternity test coming up. But I have to get this job done if I am ever going to have a career in this business. Despite working for a corporation once more, I do feel a sense of control over my work this time around."

I accepted her kisses, realizing that it was also giving me the biggest horn. I pulled her down on me and made desperate love to her again, and she let me.

Darlington axed my blog article the next day. "PMO's orders," said his terse e-mail. "All communications about the new election platform are being carefully staged from now on."

I wrote back, annoyed. "But aren't we suppose to be part of that staged communication? I thought we were on the PM's team?"

"Standby for more directives on this," was all I got back at the end of that working day from him.

I had better news to distract me from the frustration of political bureaucracy. Roy called that evening. "We can do the test tomorrow at three p.m." He gave me the address to a clinic in Hull.

"I'll be there. How are you doing?"

"I'll see you there." He clicked off.

Why was everyone being so cryptic and terse? I called Dee, and she answered her cell phone for a change. "I leave tomorrow afternoon on VIA," she announced on picking up. "This thing is moving fast."

"Oh no, not you as well," I groaned. "Why the heck is everyone in such a hurry that they are missing the common courtesies?"

"What's got into you, honey?" She sounded concerned. Then she added, "I was going to call you, but we were ironing out details until fifteen minutes ago."

I told her about Darlington and Roy. She listened, and I heard deep intakes of breath. Then she said, "Why don't we celebrate our last night in Ottawa tonight? I'll buy you dinner. At a real fancy place with great wine?"

My heart skipped. "Great! As long as it isn't at Alberto's."

We went to Enrique's instead: good South American cuisine, Argentinian pampas grown beef, a selection of Peruvian potatoes and sautéed mixed vegetables, hot peppers mixed in with the gazpacho soup, all washed down with a good bottle of Temprenillo. As the other Enrique, the handsome singer, sang his love songs over the piped music in the background, we held hands after dinner and ordered another bottle of wine. I was really mellow. I didn't care what tomorrow would bring. I just wanted to live and die in this moment.

And then it happened!

I am in the basement with the naked light bulb hanging off the ceiling swinging in the draft that comes in from somewhere, mesmerizing, drawing me to its illumination like a moth because everything else is in darkness. I, too, am naked and freezing cold. I want to enter that light and get consumed by it, for the outside is dangerous.

Then another light, from the top of the stairs, a fixed light. He is standing there. I see his heavy boots with mud on the toes. The boots start coming down the stairway, soon he is fully in view, his suspenders running over a soiled shirt. He's got the cane in his hand.

"Are you going to say you are sorry?" His voice is raspy, even bored. He has done this many times before, with many other children who have passed through his care.

"I didn't take it. Jesse did." I was told not to lie by the Jesuits at school. Lying to them brought worse punishments.

"But I found it under your pillow."

"He put it there."

A whir in the air and his stick hits my leg, bringing me to my knees. "Please, have mercy!" Another lesson taught me by the Jesuits: Christians show mercy to their fellow man.

"You will have mercy when you learn not to lie or to steal. Remember the Commandments?"

The cane comes down again, this time on my back, and there is red on the floor.

Robin Mooncroft, where are you? Come to me!

The cane is thrashing me liberally. Red is in front of my eyes. I black out before Robin can come to my rescue.

"Will! Are you all right?"

Dee's voice jerked me back from my daydream. I saw the red in front of my eyes—my glass of Temprenillo.

"I thought you were slumped into a trance," Dee was saying.

"I was." I blinked my eyes and pushed back my glass. "That will be enough wine for me for the night."

"What happened just now?"

"A blast from the past. You asked me whether I had them when I was with you. Well, I just had my first episode."

"Care to share?"

"No. Reliving it alone was scary. Let's go home. I'd rather make love than talk about my murky past."

The next afternoon, Dee left for Toronto with a huge suitcase of belongings filled with enough to last her for two months. Her paints and equipment filled another case. She faithfully agreed to keep the weekends free and send me a pack of Porter Airlines commuter air passes for me to come up for whenever I could.

That afternoon I met Roy at the clinic. The process was pretty simple. We filled out some forms, put down a credit card (mine), and provided two swabs from the insides of our cheeks. The results would be available in a week.

I took the opportunity to buy him another coffee, at Starbucks this time, and ask him about his life in foster care.

"They didn't beat me physically. That must have been in your time. Physical abuse would have gotten them put on a banned list somewhere. But psychological battering was more effective and less visible."

"Like?"

"Time outs. Being denied the things we liked—candy, movies, TV time. Pocket money withheld. Life for us was about how to cheat the system instead of how to live within it, for living within was subject to so many restrictions."

"Did you try to put the blame on others in order to escape it yourself?"

"Totally. That was how you survived. The weakest one was always the scapegoat. The plan was never to be the weakest one."

"And love? Did any of your foster parents show you love?"

"They loved the money they received to raise us. It did not come with a contract to show us any love in return. It was a business. We were the products. That's why it was easy for me to move into the escort business. I was still a product."

"Nothing much has changed there since my days in foster care. I was often the scapegoat." I felt bonded to this child by our shared miserable past.

"Let me ask you something," he said, swirling the dregs of his coffee. "If you had such a tough life as mine, how come you are working for the government and all? I've never seen anyone of my foster brothers and sisters make it past grade ten."

I had never revealed this secret recipe to anyone, but I felt Roy was deserving of it, more than even Dee. "I invented a fictional character who would rid the world of bad people. I would become this character during my bad moments—it was my escape. I also liked to read—another escape. My character's name was Robin. Robin Moorcroft, an English adventurer in France. I placed him in one of the worst periods of history—the Reign of Terror—as I felt my life was in a similar dark period. I started writing stories about him and sending them out to magazines. Those stories were an escape for me, out of my personal jail, even if they went nowhere. One of those stories won a contest, and I received a scholarship to a prestigious writing school. I was eighteen and on the cusp of being a dropout. That diploma saved my life. I wrote an entire novel about Moorcroft during the six-month course, and the school recommended me to their literary agency who sold worldwide rights of the book to a major publisher. The rest is history, as they say. . ."

"Wow, that gives me hope! I wish I had that talent."

"That run only lasted fifteen years through six novels. Then tastes changed. Now I write blogs. Nondescript, politically paid blogs in simple grammar so that they will be noticed and widely read. And it pays the bills."

"I still wish I could write or paint or play an instrument. I never had the opportunity."

"We each have different talents. Some that we discover later in life. Maybe yours is still to be discovered."

His mouth twisted cruelly. "My arse is my talent. It makes me the most money today. Letting people bugger me."

His words hurt. They cut and hurt. And I had no consolation to offer him.

"Perhaps I could help you get rid of this guy who is after you. I want to help."

"No. That would only implicate you. I don't want to dump my misery on you."

"You won't be. This is something I *want* to do for you."

"Let's wait until the test results are in. If you are indeed my father, then I will be happy to let 'Daddy' step in for a bit."

The following day, the online tabloids, the ones we called fake news and ignored, were spreading the story, and it began to trend on social media: *PM had secret talks with the Americans to take pipeline east.*

I gobbled up every link I could on this thread as this was dynamite. A direct contradiction of the new re-election platform. Apparently, the story went, while the Energy East pipeline was going through its regulatory hurdles in Quebec, our enterprising PM had conducted secret talks with the Americans to take the pipeline in a straight line through the states of New York, Vermont and New Hampshire into refineries in New Brunswick, cutting short the distance and the bureaucratic mess in La Belle Province. This was indeed dynamite! Something that, if not defused, would lead to embarrassment for our "Clean Energy PM," and a sure election loss for his party.

I phoned Darlington's office. Maddie answered. "He's not in," she said in her flat monotone.

"I didn't expect to find him. But you know where to get him quick. Tell him I called regarding the Energy East disclosure and tell him I may even have a lead on whodunit. I'm sure the PMO would be interested."

As I suspected, a message was sitting in my Twitter message box. *Hi Cunt* (not sure how I had been permanently downgraded to the female genitalia category), *watch the news on HuffPost and Breitbart this morning? Didn't I tell you the shit was going to hit the fan?*

I replied. *We may be willing to talk. To make a deal.* I had no authority to make any deals, but I was prepared to do anything to slow this juggernaut down until Darlington and his higher ups got their act together.

No response.

No response from Darlington either. By the end of the day I phoned again.

"I gave him the message soon after you called," said Maddie. "He's been closeted with the minister all day. There is turmoil on the Hill."

"I bet."

"They are trying to head off the mainstream press from running the pipeline scandal story tomorrow."

"Shit. You mean the real news is finally taking the fake news seriously?"

"Tapes of the meetings held with the Americans were sent to the Globe's offices today."

"What!"

"Yes, I told you there was trouble on the Hill."

"So, there *were* meetings with the Americans."

"Who knows? Those tapes could also have been manufactured in a studio with clever actors." Maddie's years in government service had given her wisdom beyond her looks.

"This has happened before?"

"Yes. Usually the forensics guys check out date/time stamps of the recordings and compare them against logs of the implicated parties' meetings to debunk the tapes or prove them right."

"Thanks for the information, Maddie. I'll stay in touch. If Darlington calls, I am prepared to write any counter argument or tweet to defuse the situation."

The story broke on CBC on the national news at ten o'clock that evening. Still no word from Darlington.

He called the following morning at ten. By then The Star and the Globe had already carried the story and social media was crammed.

"Sorry to be incommunicado, Smallwood. But yesterday was a heady day."

"I guess it's too late for minions like me to create any bulwark against this tsunami that's washing over us."

"Communication has been centralized with a special team in the PMO. All agencies are forbidden from writing anything."

"I guess I am out of a job then."

"Sort of. For now." I could see him smiling at the other end of the line, feeling his power over me.

"I was just getting used to this gig. Had I known this was going to happen, I may not have splurged at Alberto's the other night."

This time he laughed openly. "Welcome to government. There's never a dull moment. Stay in touch. I will e-mail when we can re-open communications."

He rang off. Ten minutes later there was a message from @abandonedchild97: *Deal? How much are you willing to pay for this.*

I replied with equal smugness: *No deal now. You released some tapes.*

His response: *I like your reference to 'You' and not to some other body out there like the Russians, Chinese or the Conservative Party, groups that everyone likes to dump on for want of a scapegoat. Now you are taking me seriously. I got more news for you. I know the hand you played in leaking those tapes.*

I was astounded. Repeat a lie often and it becomes a truth. *Me?*

Yes, you. Watch it when they tap at your door. I would get out of Dodge if I were you.

At this point, I lost interest. This guy was nuts. I un-followed him.

The next three days were miserable. With no work to do and Dee out of town, I was left kicking my heels. I decided to follow that idea I had been germinating of starting my own blog. I studied commercial bloggers. They specialized in short, fantastical stories with lots of pictures and videos and they got lots of ads in return. There were others who only acted as curators and regurgitated content from the main news sites, offering selections for special tastes; I quickly discarded this second option as I did not want to be multiplying content already in existence, the writer in me was looking to create rather than copy and paste. Then there was another type of blogger: the self-help guy—how to drive a woman crazy in bed, how to cure depression, how to achieve peak performance etc. Since I knew none of these things and was a victim of depression, nightmares, self-pity, and egomania, I discarded self-help as my path to riches. Yet, trusting that the right content would eventually come along, I decided to set up my own blog site and signed up for Google ads and Facebook ads and other companies that had been sending me ad requests in the past that I had been ignoring. I went to Wordpress and set up a vanilla site and added some standard templates, then played with some fancy fonts until I came up with one that looked distinct. I tried over fifty different selfie shots until I found one half decent and added it to the site. All this kept me busy during my forced redundancy.

Now, what was I going to use for content? Could I serialize my books and post them for free? Hmm! they were kind of dated and my publishers might have a fit. Even though they made very little money off me now, my publishers still had proprietary copyright on my work. Wouldn't the advertisers also have a say in my copy and choose to place their ads where the copy complimented the advertisements and the products they featured? This was sounding rather complicated. So, to avoid any copyright issues, I posted my visit to the yoga retreat as a Proustian episode, with real names amended to protect the innocent and the villains, ending that chapter with a "to be continued" banner. I sprinkled some photos I had taken at the retreat with my cell phone camera to spice up the article—after all we were in the Instagram age. Then I placed the Google ads logo on it. *Now, let it go. Villainy thou art afoot!*

I began to study the advertisements on blog sites and tried to match them against the articles appearing next to them. It was obvious that the ads were matched to my profile and that the corresponding news article had nothing to do with it. And the more sites I searched and the more articles I read, the more my online search profile began changing. The ads were following me. To test the theory, I went to a few X-rated sites and then to a general news site, and I immediately started getting served up with men's club ads and penis enlargement inducements. It took more benign searches before the Cialis and Viagra ads fell off. I figured my yoga retreat episode would appeal to those in mid-life crisis looking for an answer, and to those looking for hope, and hopefully there were a lot of those people around.

I distracted myself in between my blog work by following the PM scandal on the news and on social media. The latest reports said that there was no conclusive evidence of the date the tape was made, for no date/time stamps were available, nor could they be determined due to the equipment that had been used. One thing was clear, it wasn't a government tape. The voices on the recording were not distinct either as the recorder appeared to have been held at some distance, probably smuggled inside someone's clothing, so that it was debatable if it was really the PM on tape. The PMO issued a severe denial, and the PM himself went on national TV on the third night after the story broke to emphatically deny that such meetings with the Americans had taken place and to reaffirm his commitment to the environment. He had also launched an investigation into the matter and promised that "perpetrators would be dealt with expeditiously."

By Day Three, I was ready to climb the wall. Dee had faithfully e-mailed me six passes on Porter to use whenever, and I was thinking of visiting. I was missing her. I phoned and asked whether I could come and informed her that my work had come to a standstill in light of the PM scandal.

"If I were Darlington, I'd be mounting a vigorous anti-pipeline response in social media," she said on the phone. "I thought you would have been worked off your feet at the moment."

"Maybe our team lacks credibility. Or perhaps the PMO is running scared and wants to keep a tighter control. We've had our share of loose cannons in government in the past."

As she was very busy with her new team, we agreed that I would visit Toronto in two days, the Friday of that week.

The following morning, Thursday at six thirty a.m., there was a pounding on my front door. Pulling on a dressing gown I stumbled towards the noise and peeped through the spy hole. One of my mad tweeter's last tweets instantly crossed my mind when I saw the two men in trench coats standing outside.

Watch it when they tap at your door.

I relaxed when I saw that one of the men was Darlington. But here? How did he know where I lived? Employment contract records, perhaps. But this early in the morning? He must be needing my help, finally. I felt vindicated.

I opened the door and looked upon him triumphantly.

"Hello, professor. What a surprise! Needing emergency services?" I was trying to sound ebullient, but my voice was hoarse.

He looked a bit embarrassed, even paternal. "Can we talk inside?" he asked.

I showed them in with a swoop of my hand. "Come on in, I'll make coffee."

"No, we have no time for that. This is Special Agent Coteau from CSIS."

Coteau nodded. He was the prototype of a burly cop, with a bushy salt and pepper mustache—ex RCMP, I surmised. The panic started coming back.

Darlington looked around my apartment, and his eyes settled on my laptop lying on the dining room table where I had been doing all my personal blog work. He cleared his throat. "Are we alone in here?"

"Yes."

"Good. I'll make this quick. This concerns the investigation being conducted by the PMO. I have instructions to hand over certain outside government contractors' laptops and other communications devices to CSIS. Can we have your department laptop and cell phone, please?"

A cold vice gripped my heart.

"Sure, " I stammered. "But the cell phone is my private one. I didn't rate high enough for a departmental phone."

Coteau spoke up in a thick French accent. "We'll take your personal phone too, Monsieur Smallwood. There are more communications on cell phones than on laptops these days. Everything will be returned after the search."

"And how long do I go without a cell phone?"

"That depends," Coteau said moving towards the laptop.

"Wait a second," I blocked his path. "Am I now a suspect?"

"Everyone is a suspect, Smallwood," Darlington said from over Coteau's shoulder. "Until this matter is cleared up. I hope you will not make this difficult for us. I asked Monsieur Coteau to leave his assistants, ahem…police officers, in the car downstairs for I knew you would co-operate."

"Like hell I would. Do you have a warrant for seizing my stuff?"

"It's not a seizure, it's a search. You are interested in keeping your job after this is over, aren't you, Smallwood?"

"Stuff the job! You can take the laptop; it belongs to the government. But you will not take the phone."

"Worried we will transcribe all your calls with the lady of Divine Secrets?" I saw malice cross Darlington's face for the first time.

"That's none of your business. Now take the laptop and go and let me get back to sleep."

Darlington nodded at Coteau who went over to the table and pulled out the laptop with its power chord.

"Mr. Smallwood," the special agent said, wrapping the cord around the laptop, "Until you hear back from us, I suggest you do not leave Ottawa."

"So now it's house arrest as well?" I was getting really mad and was at the point of losing it.

"No. But if we find anything we need clarification on, we will be back."

"You can phone me. I still have a cell phone, remember? Do you want me to write down the number?"

"That won't be necessary," Darlington said. "We have your contact information back at the office. That hasn't changed, has it?"

"No. But I take it, my employment status with you has now changed, seeing that I have failed to fully co-operate."

Darlington took a deep breath and exhaled. The paternal look re-appeared. "Smallwood, we understand this has been rather sudden and intrusive for you. We understand the anger and irritation this visit must have provoked. If nothing else is found in our search, we will be back to business as usual and all outbursts that went on inside here will be forgotten. I am sorry to have sounded heavy handed myself."

Carrying my government-issue laptop, they exited quickly. From the window, I saw a police cruiser merge into traffic.

I cursed myself for having done all my recent work on the office laptop due to its superior performance, and not on my old clunker that had been unused since I got the government job. Given that I had a social media function, my access too on that government owned machine had been unrestricted as I was expected to scour the internet for material and for trending stories.

Well, at least my cell phone was safe, and the log of calls between me and Dee was out of Darlington's prying eyes, although I knew it was no big deal for them to get a telephone log these days, if they wanted one.

Then I had a panic attack. I was not the only one in danger. Roy was too. Even though he was not involved and no longer had control over the Twitter handle, @abandonedchild97 was plastered all over that laptop, his Twitter feed had been bookmarked, along with the incriminating porno sites and all.

I phoned him. I got voicemail. He must be sleeping it off after a late shift at some part time job or after a visit to a client the night before. My skin crawled at the thought.

My arse is my talent.

I left him a message to call me urgently. Then I realized that if my cell phone was confiscated, he would be traceable too.

I went at noon to his restaurant at ByWard market. I bypassed the maitre d' and walked right up to Roy. He was setting up glasses on a counter.

"The results are not out yet," he said, looking up at me, protesting before I could even open my mouth.

"It's not about that. CSIS is onto @abandonedchild97 for the government pipeline scandal. You could be implicated."

His hand rose to his mouth, and his eyes widened. "What?" he said, lowering his hand.

"You need to cancel that account ASAP. Write to Twitter, say that someone is using it. Set up a trail that will exonerate you."

"It's too late. It will look like an excuse from the culprit if I do it now."

He was right.

"Do it anyway. It's better than doing nothing. And when you call me in future use a payphone or someone else's phone. My cell phone is going to be seized by CSIS any time now."

The maitre d' was coming towards me with a scowl on his face, so I left Roy standing, darted around some other tables, and escaped through the front door. I hoped Roy didn't get into trouble with his boss for my breach of protocol.

Chapter 8

I froze outside my building—upon returning from meeting Roy—when I saw the police cruiser parked at the front door. They were back. They must have found something that piqued their interest. And this time my cell phone was sure to be confiscated. There was no way I was going inside, so I slunk away, down two streets, rounding the corner until my neighborhood bank came into view. I hurried inside the bank and withdrew my maximum daily allowance of $500. That should hold me for awhile. I was running on adrenaline. And I wasn't thinking all that straight. I hailed a cab and asked the driver to take me to the airport.

Something told me that running was futile. These days, with surveillance what it was, it would only be a matter of time, perhaps hours, before they picked me up. Even now, the airport could be under watch for me. But my survival instinct said I needed to run, get away. That's what had kept me ahead of all those predators who had paraded as caregivers in my childhood.

I gave the friendly airline clerk my name and said that there were several passes in my name, and could she find them on her computer. After several tries, and a call to the Toronto office, she located them and booked me on the six p.m. flight, leaving in two hours. Would the cops check out the airport in the meantime? Or would they merely post a watch outside my apartment until they realized that I wasn't coming back. Those two hours at the airport were an agony. I fully expected "Wanted Dead or Alive" signs with my mug shot being posted everywhere inside the terminal. I finally spent the last half hour locked up in one of the men's washroom cubicles and making a dash for my flight only when its final announcement was made.

We took off without incident, and I wondered whether I was blowing this all out of proportion. For now, I was plagued by further anxieties. I was going to Toronto, a place I hadn't voluntarily been to in twenty years, except for the odd book launch, reading, or literary festival that I had been mandatorily expected to attend by my publisher, until those "appearances" had mercifully tailed off in recent years. Toronto held only bad memories: of growing up, of Jacqueline, of a struggle with no reward. I tried to offset these negative thoughts by thinking of Dee. Dee was in Toronto, and I was going to her. She was the only refuge I had. Then I panicked again. I had the cops on my tail, and I would be dragging Dee and her re-invigorated career into this mess. I couldn't do that to her.

When the plane landed at the island airport, I called her cell. From the terminal building I could see the Royal Excelsior Hotel peeking out from between the tall buildings on the other side of the narrow strip of water. Toronto was no longer the city I had once known, the topography had changed; from what I could see it was no longer a clean, mini-Manhattan; it was a full blown one—dirt, congestion and all.

Thankfully, I got her on my third try.

"I'm busy," she sounded annoyed when she finally picked up.

"I'm here," I said.

"A day early? I thought you were coming tomorrow evening. I've got to work tomorrow."

"Listen to me. This is a matter of national importance." Before she could protest, I recounted the visits from Darlington and the police. She remained quiet during my spiel, interrupting only with sharp intakes of breath from time to time. I ended by saying, "I don't want to implicate you by coming over there, but at the time I could only thinking of running to you. What do I do?"

"You have to come to my hotel, of course. You can stay here until we sort this out. Don't go to the reception. I should be back in an hour. Come up to Room 1005 at seven thirty p.m. I'll leave the door unlocked.

Now I have to run off and finish here so I can get to the hotel in time. And don't do anything stupid in the meantime."

Her take-charge attitude re-assured me. I melted into the streets of Toronto for the next hour. Everything had compacted due to the tall buildings that had sprung up in the intervening years and others that were still under construction, overshadowing the finite old streets that looked narrow and tired. Facades of historic buildings had been removed and lay on what used to be bus and bike lanes as their main structures were being raised, shrinking the streets even more. People walked faster. The mosaic had become the melting pot with a distinct characteristic: people were in a hurry and rude. And everyone was buried in their smart phones plugged into earphones: the overworked masses who gobbled up social media to hide from the emptiness of their lives, the masses I was blogging for.

That reminded me to check out my personal blog article I had posted the day before. I dived into a Tim Horton's where free WiFi was available, grabbed a sandwich, and checked out the blog on my phone. The site was slow. When I eventually reached it, I couldn't believe what I was seeing: the article had received over a thousand reads and several comments, and the ads had started appearing on it. This was more hits in twenty-four hours than any of my government blogs had ever attracted. Had I gone viral? The depression of the last twenty-four hours lifted. More likely, I had hit some kind of new paydirt! People liked this shit I was writing, it seemed. And they liked it in the digestible bites that I was serving up, not in entire novels that never got read to their ends because people were walking fast and hooked into their smart phones. My new stuff was being consumed off those very smart phones! I had discovered my new kind of fiction!

I finished my sandwich, dragged myself away from reading the glowing comments on my blog, and headed for my appointment with Dee. As I was exiting Timmy's, my phone rang. I looked at caller ID: unknown.

Like a hypnotized subject, I pressed the "take call" button and listened.

"Smallwood. Smallwood is that you? Hello! Answer, man!" It was Darlington.

Stupid of me to think I could escape with the very homing device that would bring them to me. Now they would know I was in Toronto. I dismissed the call and shut the phone off. I walked down to the water again and tossed the phone into the flotsam of Lake Ontario. Then I headed north for the Royal Excelsior.

I steered well clear of the reception area and took the elevator to Room 1005 which was to be my new home for the indeterminate future.

I barely recognized Dee in her corporate suit when she opened the door for me. I gasped and stared. Where was the earthy hippy woman I had first been drawn to, one epitomizing freedom, individuality and bravado? With a stray hair or two escaping a tight bun she had pulled her hair into, and traces of heavy makeup starting to wear out at day's end, she was encased in corporate conformity, and the hotel suite containing her put the seal on it.

"What are you staring at?" she asked in the doorway. The room behind her held a writing desk, TV and a small dining table and chairs. A doorway at the other end led into another room, the bedroom. I figured that the suites in these old colonial hotels were larger than modern apartments, so we were not going to be too crowded inside here.

"You."

"Coming in?"

"I am reluctant. I come bearing much baggage."

"Oh, come off it." She grabbed me by the hand and pulled me inside, slamming the door with her other hand. We hugged, passion overcoming remoteness. I felt her insistence to have me inside her, and I took great pleasure in walking her backwards across the outer room into the bedroom and peeling that unwelcome suit and other accoutrements off her body until she was stark naked. I pulled out the pins that held her hair up and let her tresses fall over her shoulders. I raised her hands above her head and kissed her shaved armpits, missing only the fragrant fuzz that used to be there.

After we had satiated our lust for each other, we lay cradled in each other's arms. However, I sensed a tenseness that had not quite left her body, unlike on previous occasions of post-coital bliss.

"Want some more loving, honey?" I said, my rapier winding up for a repeat performance.

She sat up, pulling the bed sheets around her. "No. This thing with Darlington. I think I may have caused it."

I sat up too. "How?" My erection wilted.

She rose from the bed, dropping the sheet and walking naked across this functional bedroom with its king-sized bed and bench at the foot end, its mirrored dresser and giant glass wardrobe doors that introduced kink into our sex, and into the en-suite bathroom. She returned with a white hotel-crested bathrobe around her.

"I told you how Darlington was after me at the yoga resort, didn't I? You saw how mad he was when we left, dashing that camera into smithereens and all."

"I still have nightmares over it."

"Well, at about the time I was interviewing for this job, he contacted me again and apologized."

"You didn't tell me that part."

"He also offered to get you a job in government as a peace offering."

"So, the 'influential cousin twice removed' was a piece of fiction?"

"I made it up because if I told you it had been Darlington your pride may have forced you to reject the offer at the time."

"Is there anything else you are not telling me? That perhaps you and Darlington were in cahoots trying to set me up as a patsy?" I was getting angry at this new information. "Let's throw in the guru as well. Let's make the retreat a recruitment centre for fall guys."

Tears came into her eyes. She came over to the bed and knelt down at my feet, looking up into my eyes. "Please, darling. I know you have a right to be mad at me. But I didn't think things would get to this. I was merely trying to help. And I thought he was too. I am not in cahoots with anyone but you."

Now it was my turn to get up and pace the breadth of the room. I am normally shy when it comes to exposing my nudity, even to Dee, but this time I was lost in thought and unselfconscious. "I'm sure he is going to trace you to this hotel and come calling. During our conversations he has always enquired after you, and I foolishly let him know that we were still together."

"You must stay here. In fact, this is the best place to hang out for anonymity. I have two keys, and you can have one. Come and go without attracting attention. Stay out of the room between ten a.m. and noon for that's when the maid comes in. I usually order room service for dinner, and that meal is sufficient for two."

"This is all well and good. But it is only short term. Long term I need to make my own case. And with my cell phone residing at the bottom of Lake Ontario and a laptop that could be loaded with all sorts of phony data in his hands, I'm a sitting duck."

"I can get you a spare phone and a new laptop."

"I have no money, other than the four hundred and seventy-five left from my last bank withdrawal. Any plastic card transactions can be traced."

"Don't worry about that. I think I have enough for both of us for now."

"A kept man."

"Writers were always kept men."

"We called that having a benefactor or a sponsor."

"Well, call it what you like."

There was tap at the door making both of us jump.

"Hide in the bathroom," Dee whispered and tightened the bathrobe around her. "I'll get the door."

I ran into the bathroom and kept the door open a crack to hear what was going on outside. I felt so trapped: naked and on the run. I was like a character from one of my historical novels with Robespierre's goons after him.

Dee's voice was clear from the doorway but the other voice, a familiar deep male voice, was muffled.

"I am sorry he is not here," Dee was saying. "He lives in Ottawa."

Mumble…mumble…mumble…I searched my memory for that other baritone voice.

"I'm sorry I cannot give that to you. I don't know who you are, and that information is confidential. Now if you will excuse me, I have a bath waiting," Dee said, voice artificially raised. The front door slammed. Moments later she slipped into the bathroom, leaned against the door, and exhaled.

I gave a her a moment to compose herself.

"Russian guy. Gave his name as Boris Lasky. Says he is a journalist. He was looking for you."

"Did he say which newspaper?"

"No."

"Then he is not a journalist."

And then it hit me. The voice. It was the man in Alberto's who had been with Darlington that evening. Igor.

My forced exile at the Royal Excelsior got underway, and I developed a routine that would make me invisible to everyone but Dee. I escaped the maid by scooting out when she went in to do the first room by the elevator. Dee's room was midway so there was no way she would stop by it first. I never went by the reception area or spoke to the doormen. I bought some spare clothes, paying cash, and used a laundromat down the street to keep them clean. For meals, it was Timmy's by day and room service at night. After a week, I started to get bored.

Dee did her best to keep me engaged. On the first day of my stay, she bought me a phone and a laptop as promised, and I got myself re-connected with the world with fake addresses and IDs. These being the latest models since I had bought clunkier versions eons ago, the new laptop looked like a thin notepad from the outside, and the phone looked like a pack of gum—sleek. But they each packed more memory and RAM than five of my old versions. The only people whom I gave my new phone number to were Dee and Roy, and I memorized their numbers without storing them on the phone. I resumed surfing to the places I used to frequent in cyberspace—Facebook, Twitter, my blog, my e-mail accounts—and checked out if anything had moved. I found my government IDs had been deleted. My blog had surpassed all expectations, and there were now requests for the second episode from more than a few readers. At this rate revenue must be trickling into my PayPal account. I checked it and, yes, $248.34 had already been deposited. But I dared not pull the money out or transfer it to my bank in case it left another trail.

On Day Five of my stay at the hotel there was a news report that alleged bribes had been paid to middlemen to bring the US pipeline players to those secret meetings the PM was supposed to have been engaged in. The report had been originally filed in one of the dubious news sites but journalists from the legit news media were now investigating. Question Period in Parliament had seen the same question raised, and the PM was observed to clear his throat a lot while providing a denial of all knowledge. A snap poll conducted the following day showed the PM's popularity had slipped a full ten points since the pipeline scandal broke.

There was still no co-ordinated media response from the PMO. On Day Seven, a news story broke on the Morning Show: government security services were investigating a hacker in the Environment Ministry who was reputed to have provided sensitive information to foreign agents trying to disrupt the upcoming spring election that the PM had called. Now there was doubt as to whether the early election call had been an unwise move and whether the schedule should have been left for the original fall time frame. By noon that day they even had an ID on the hacker: my photo was being proudly flashed on news screens across the country.

A vice gripped my heart when I looked at my likeness staring back at me—the same mug shot from my government ID badge. I began to panic and paced the suite, muttering, swearing, and on the brink of tears. Now I couldn't even go outside in daylight hours. I had compromised Dee by hiding out here. I had to leave. But go where?

As I paced the room, I tried to get my rational mind working above the panic that threatened to engulf me. Was I being framed? Why? What was so damned bad that I had done? I hadn't killed anyone. I hadn't slandered the PM or his government. But that was only provable if I had my laptop with me. What had been planted on it after it had been taken away? What search history, what fake documents, e-mail strings? And whose side was Darlington on?

But wait a second. If I got caught and was handed over to the police, technically this smear campaign would end, right? The culprit would have been caught. I would tell my story, the attention would shift to my case, and the PM would be absolved and be free to pursue his re-election campaign. My getting caught would upset the bad guys' plans, whoever those bad guys were—government, Darlington, the Russians or some yet unnamed agency.

My cell phone rang. It was Dee, so I picked it up.

"Have you seen the news?" I asked her without even pausing to say hello.

"Yes," Her voice was muted. "I don't want you running away. I'm leaving early. I should be there in an hour."

"You should not be seen with me."

"I want to be with you. If they want to come and catch you, then I want to be there."

"I need to turn myself in. Tell them my side of the story and clear up this whole mess."

"That's what I was thinking. We'll go to the police together."

I promised to wait until she got here.

As soon as she rang off, the phone went off again. It was Roy.

"You're famous," he said. He sounded breathless. "Infamous."

"Thank you. Want my autograph?"

"What'll you do?"

"I'm going to make a full confession. I did nothing wrong."

"Well, you certainly *did* something wrong at my end."

"What?"

"The clinic called."

I'd forgotten entirely about the DNA test.

Roy continued, and his voice sounded strained. "The results were in ahead of schedule. I didn't know when you'd get back to Ottawa, so I went there myself."

"And...?" *Pray God, I don't need another catastrophe.*

"And you *are* my daddy. Hello, Daddy!"

I collapsed on the bed. "You picked a helluva time to tell me that."

"Did you pick a good time to dump me? When I was an infant?" The hysteria had returned to his voice, like when I had first cornered him in the restaurant at the ByWard Market.

"Listen. I am sorry for all that has happened, okay? Your mother was a basket case, okay? One moment I was the father, the next moment I wasn't, then I was, and on it went. There was a whole lot of shit going on at that time. And I was not ready to be a father." But deep down inside me, despite my protests, jubilation was gurgling. I had a son.

"Blame it on my mother, then. She's not around to answer, is she? It's all about you, isn't it?"

"No, it's all about *you*. We are peas in a pod. Self-absorbed narcissists."

We were shouting at each other.

And then someone pounded on the door.

I dropped my voice. "I have to go. Will call you later." I rung off and switched the phone off in case he called again to pile more guilt on me.

I tucked the phone into the calf pocket of my jeans and tiptoed towards the front door. To my horror, I saw it opening, the maid having used her passkey to gain access. She stepped aside politely and ushered in the man behind her. Igor.

Igor entered in a rush, bowed to the maid and spoke in Russian, extending a twenty-dollar bill. Then he almost pushed her out and closed the door.

"What the—!" was all I managed to get out at this intrusion before he swung around and caught me with a roundhouse to the side of the head that saw lights go off around me, dropping me back onto the sofa.

I struggled to orient myself. Blurrily I saw him pull something out of his jacket and stick it in my ribs. The metal hurt me, and I flinched. I was still having trouble focussing, and I felt the side of my head going numb.

"Listen, you prick," Igor said, and his last word sounded like "brick." "We are going for a ride."

Then I was being hauled to my feet. I was unsteady, so I let myself slump, supported by his grasp on my collar. He pushed me into the corridor where two other suited men stood. The maid had vanished, so had her cart. Between the three men, who propped me up by keeping me in the middle, they marched me down the empty corridor. They were Russians, for they mumbled between themselves in that language as they frog marched me into the elevator and down to street level, then through the side doors into a limo purring by the swinging doors of the hotel exit. All this time we hadn't encountered a single soul. Was this city dead? I thought of running as we hit the street and emerged into the usual crush of people, but that metal prod of Igor's that hadn't left my side dissuaded me. Besides, everyone was plugged into their smart phones. Who the heck would have the time or interest in me? One of Igor's men got into the limo first, and I was shoved into the middle of the back seat with the second man following behind me. Igor got in the front passenger seat, and the driver took off even before all the vehicle's doors closed.

Then I felt a prick on my arm and realized too late that the guy who had come in behind had just shot a hypodermic into my shoulder. The results were almost instantaneous. My hazy eyesight became fogged and my ears thundered. My mouth went dry, and I couldn't stifle the yawning that burst out from me. Before we hit the Gardiner Expressway, I was fast asleep.

Chapter 9

I woke up with a splitting headache. My throat was dry. I was on a bed in what looked like another hotel room, and the blinds in the window were drawn. Through a partially closed door I heard a television set blaring in the next room.

I tried to get out of the bed and realized that one of my legs was tied to the bed post with a nylon rope. Whoever had done that was an idiot. They'd left my hands untied. As I reached down to untie my leg, I struck something hard in my jeans pocket. My new cellphone. The imbeciles hadn't confiscated that either. My confidence was starting to build. I untied my leg with no difficulty, stepped off the bed, and inched towards the door. The frikking door creaked as I pulled it open a bit more to get a view outside. Ah, that must have been their warning signal. Igor's two goons were in this outer room, the living room of a hotel suite, I gathered, smaller than Dee's and shabbier. One goon had his back to me, sitting on the sofa watching a blue movie. The TV screen facing me showed a woman getting gang banged by a bunch of burly men, pretending to enjoy what she was doing. The other guy had positioned himself on a stool sideways between the TV screen and bedroom door and immediately saw me peeping through.

He rose, panic crossing his face and pulled out a pistol, shouting, "*Davai, davai!*"

His companion jumped off the sofa and swivelled around, and, other than for the bulge in his fly, he too had a firearm pointed at me.

I put my hands up and yelled. "Don't shoot!"

The porn watcher strode up to me, grabbed me by the shoulder and dragged me into the living room. He pushed me into the armchair to the left of the sofa and shouted, *"Syad."*

I sat. They resumed their seats, Porno Guy to my right and Other Guy facing me on the stool. I guess they needed me where they could watch me and their movie as well. I was forced to watch their sordid film which gave them many a chuckle, especially when the male studs came in the woman's mouth, and the cum looked like something squeezed out of a tube of toothpaste, too white and creamy for the real stuff but highly distinguishable on the screen. When the first movie ended another started, I realized that this must be a twenty-four-hour X-rated stream purchased off the hotel's video channel. Was I going to have to watch this writhing meat market for my entire stay?

"Can we watch the news?" I ventured. What did I have to lose?

Porno Guy frowned at me, then spoke in accented English. "No news for you. Only sex movie. You like?"

So, they understood English.

"No." I replied flatly and shook my head.

They laughed.

The next movie was more of the same with a twist. Women dressed as nuns were having sex with a stud dressed in a cassock, and he seemed to be overwhelmed at first and then rose to the occasion with gusto. Soon the altar boys and the sacristan had joined in, and an orgy had begun with lots of sacrificial wine being poured over naked bodies. The depravity was beginning to sicken me, but the goons were engrossed.

"Can I have some water?" I asked.

The guy on the stool gestured to the mini bar in the corner of the room. "Drink."

I went over and found a bottle of water in the fridge and drank it gratefully. Water dribbled down my chin in my haste. A few napkins were stacked nearby, and I picked one up. It had a logo on it, but I tried not to call attention by trying to decipher it in these goons' presence, so I stuffed it into my pocket after drying my hands. I returned to my chair and lay my head back. The waves of sleep hadn't quite left, and I felt myself dozing. Mercifully, I didn't have to watch more copulating bodies, but I couldn't shut my ears from the grunts, squeals and evenly spaced uttering of "fuck me" by the horny actors.

As I drifted in and out of sleep, my mind started working again. I was obviously being held prisoner but was not in imminent danger, even though my minders were armed. Were these guys part of Darlington's organization or were they rivals? Were these the same guys who were trying to disrupt the election like they had done in the USA three years ago? Why had they left my phone with me? Sloppiness? Or had they taken its battery out? And where the hell was I?

I figured out a game plan based on the assumption that these guys were inept minders doing a job they didn't really want to do.

I rose from my chair and yawned. "Sleep," I said and rested my head sideways in my clasped hands. I pointed to the bedroom and repeated the gesture.

Porno Guy nodded, *"Davai."* I had taken by now that they used the word *"davai"* for a lot of things, mostly acceptable things. The unacceptable was *"nyet."* As I walked towards the bedroom, I heard the first *"nyet."* I stopped and turned. Porno Guy had pulled a set of handcuffs and was approaching me. He pushed me into the bedroom, then onto the bed, and slipped one cuff over my right hand and fastened the other one to the bed pole.

"Davai," he said with satisfaction. He even pulled out a blanket from the closet and threw it to me to cover myself. Then he returned to his movie leaving the light on in the bedroom.

"Can you shut the door, please? Or turn the volume down," I called after him.

A hand gripped the door and pulled it from the other side. The door was shut between me and them. Great!

I tried moving in the bed. My free left hand could reach the phone in my pocket. I hauled it out and checked; the battery was still in and it had about 30% of power left. Enough to get an emergency call out, but I dare not switch it on in case it beeped and farted, or heavens forbid, all stacked text messages from the time I had been kidnapped poured in making all sorts of vibrations and bell rings. I slipped the phone under my pillow and tried standing up and reaching for the window. I cracked the blinds and looked out. It was dark already, and the clear skyline of a city looked back at me. Was this the same night of the day I had been kidnapped or several nights later? I scanned the horizon and my heart leaped. Was that the tip of the CN tower I saw in the distance, standing above all else? By my estimation of where I was looking out from, we had to be east of the city. Perhaps somewhere northeast, like in Oshawa. I pulled out the used napkin and smoothed it on my pillow. The Rainbow Inn, it said, no address. That was all I had to work with. This was when I kicked myself for not getting familiar with Google Maps and its location services. But now I had no battery power or time to fiddle with Google.

I switched the phone on under the pillow and checked quickly for volume, ringtones, vibration levels etc., and turned them all off. There were several text messages, but I didn't bother to check them—later, if battery power held. One of those guys could peep his head in through the door any minute now.

Who should I call? 911? Yeah right and start answering a myriad of questions before the cops got here. Besides, I was a wanted man. They'd put me down to a crank if I gave them my name. I wasn't going to phone Dee. I had put her in enough trouble already. Roy. My son. He was my only hope. I would text him as voices would carry.

I typed a quick note to him. "Kidnapped and being held in The Rainbow Inn north of Oshawa somewhere. Can you find me? Will check back in a few minutes."

Then I thought of Dee. She must have returned to the hotel by now, found me gone, and must be worried out of her mind. Would she have gone to the police as she had intended to?

I wondered why I hadn't sent her the same message I had sent Roy. What if Roy didn't even get my text?

I quickly reverted to the phone to send Dee a text message as well when I saw a new one flash across the screen. It was from Roy.

"Checked Google Maps. The Rainbow Inn is now called the Delawana Inn, new management, Russian company. In Whitby. Give me more info."

I poured out a lengthy description involving the kidnapping at the Royal Excelsior, the two henchman, Igor, porn movies, and the fact that I was handcuffed to a bed. When I had emptied my brain, I hit send. Then I slid the phone under my pillow. There was only about twenty percent of power remaining. I decided not to send a message to Dee—it wouldn't serve any purpose than to distress her more.

Just as well too, for the door opened and Porno Guy stuck his head in. I pretended to be asleep, lying on my back with eyes slatted up at the ceiling. He was on his phone as he surveyed me from head to foot. Finally, he nodded, left the door half open and went back to his movie.

I rolled on my side with my back to the half open door, slid the phone from under the pillow and read it. The message from Roy made my heart leap. "Got it. I am on my way."

Then I panicked. Roy was on his way? Here? I had never asked him to stick his neck out for me. I had assumed he would go to the police. Risking discovery, I slid the phone out again and typed, "Call the police. Don't put yourself at risk."

The reply. "The last people I need are the cops. I'm known to them here. . .in my line of work. They won't believe me."

I switched off the phone and tucked it beneath the mattress this time. I gave up. *Now let it work, villainy thou art afoot!*

I must have fallen asleep. More nightmares, but this time there were priests and nuns stripping and running naked all over the place, fornicating behind bushes and anywhere they damned well pleased, and it was more enjoyable and funny and literally a "*fucking* nightmare." I awoke with a full bladder and a hard on. The outer room was quiet, the TV was off. I heard snores from out there, two kinds, my guards were asleep. But I couldn't get out of this handcuff. And I needed to pee badly. So, I began shouting.

"Hey. Wake up guys. I need to take a piss."

One set of snoring stopped in a choking gurgle, like an engine sputtering down before switching off, a chair groaned, and a moment later Porno Guy stuck his head in the door. "*Davai?*"

"No *Davai,*" I said. "Piss." I gesticulated at my crotch.

"*Karashow.*" He nodded and advanced into the room. His shirt was half out of his pants and his blond hair was tousled. Talking of crotches, his fly was undone, and the front of his pants were stained. Too many movies, I gathered.

He unlocked my handcuff and gestured for me to go to the bathroom. He stood outside while I peed. I looked around for a sharp object to whack him with when I came out, but there was none. I didn't like the idea of Roy getting here with these two guys and their pistols. It was also the thought of those pistols that made me abandon my thought of trying to get away or of whacking any of them. I washed and wiped my hands and exited the bathroom. I was re-cuffed to the bed and Porno Guy went out, mercifully switching off the bedroom light this time. I must have fallen asleep like a light too. No priests and nuns this time.

When I woke, my minders were in a better mood. They unlocked me and ushered me into the living room where a breakfast of bacon, eggs and toast awaited, replete with orange juice. I didn't ask questions but ate ravenously. My guards were content to drink repetitive cups of coffee from the coffeemaker by the bar.

"You want see news?" Porno Guy asked me. Without waiting for my answer, he switched on the TV and surfed channels to CBC. He gave his companion a glance.

The date stamp on the news channel confirmed what I had seen on my phone. It was two days after my kidnapping, so I hadn't been gone long, but a lot had happened in the meantime. The scandal surrounding the PM was now national news. Bribes and cover ups were the new twist in this story. Twitter feeds scrolling at the bottom showed how irate the electorate was with this perceived failed attempt at "selling out to the Americans" that had now been outed. Members of both the government and the opposition were being polled for comments, but the common thread from everyone was how much was coming to light so quickly. Where had all this stuff been hiding, or, as I would have liked to know, where was it being manufactured now that I, the so-called perpetrator, was no longer working?

And the news about the counter investigation about the hacker was being touted by all media as another cover-up by the PMO to deflect attention from the pipeline scandal. The bad guys were winning in the public opinion polls, it appeared.

I felt drowsy after my big breakfast, but I knew that I needed to keep my body moving if something was going to happen today following Roy's braggadocious responses last night. So, I started pacing the living room. My minders gave me interested looks and then dismissed me as not likely a flight risk. Promptly after the morning news finished, Porno Guy flipped to his favourite channel, and I was assailed by a fresh round of male and female genitalia that competed for the Guinness Book of Records under the longest, biggest, strongest and fullest categories, grinding it out with gasps, squeals, "fuck-mes" and oodles of toothpaste.

I focussed on pacing faster, getting my heart rate up and tuning out the racket on the boob tube. I concentrated on what I had heard over the morning newscast. Whoever was masterminding the disinformation campaign was choreographing it artfully. First the bombshell about the

PM and pipelines (alleged culprit: me), then the follow up leaks and social media noise on bribes, cover-ups and cover-ups of the cover-ups. This was textbook "How to Sabotage an Election" and live to tell the tale.

If I could just escape these two porn addicts and make it to the nearest police station to tell them my story, perhaps after the authorities got past their incredulity and after my bona fides had been checked out, they might believe me and this evil tide might start to turn. But how to escape? Despite their apparent incompetence, these two guys had me covered. And those guns they carried scared me. Then through my concentration I heard another noise competing with the television sex orgy: the doorbell was ringing.

My two minders, whose tumescence was now showing, looked at each other, frowning. Porno Guy pulled out his pistol, and his companion shook his hand furiously saying, *"Nyet, nyet!"*

Keeping his pistol at the ready behind his back, Porno Guy advanced on the door and looked out of the peephole. He started coughing at what he saw. Grabbing the handle, he wrenched open the door. A strangled "Ah!" escaped him.

Framed in the doorway, in a long red dress, low cut with a bosom to die for, stood my former lover and nemesis, Jacqueline.

Now it was my turn to go "Ah!" and jump back a step from the direction in which I had been pacing. Jacqueline? WTF!

But "Jacqueline" was not paying me the slightest attention. She had her eyes on Porno Guy. She spoke to him in Russian and caressed his cheeks. He grabbed her by the hand and dragged her into the suite, kicking the door shut behind her. Then he said something to Other Guy. Other Guy replied in anger. Porno Guy stamped his foot and dragged Jacqueline over to the bedroom I had just exited and slammed the door behind them. Other Guy shrugged and returned to his stool. He pointed to the chair I had been sitting on and shouted, *"Syad!"* He looked pissed. He took out his pistol and laid it across his knees for emphasis.

Sounds from the bedroom indicated that a porno show of another sort was commencing. Jacqueline was squealing and shouting "fuck me" and Porno Guy was panting, and Other Guy started cranking up the volume of the fake fuck show on TV to drown out the real one on the other side of the wall.

Being closer to the bedroom than Other Guy, I heard more of what was going on in the real show. I was also more interested in that show, for who the heck was this mystery woman? Then it hit me, just as I heard Porno Guy come with a giant "Arrrrr!" There was a thud that shook the room. Even Other Guy heard it and jumped up, advancing towards the bedroom door with gun outstretched.

I acted quickly. "They are busy. Do not disturb."

Other Guy looked hesitant. Just then the bedroom creaked open (damn that creak, it reminded me of being in a Hitchcock movie!) Jacqueline stood in the doorway, still in her red dress but with her hair dishevelled and her eyes looking fevered, raunchy. In her hand she dangled a pair of panties. Her other hand remained behind her back. Twirling the panties, hers, I took it, she advanced on Other Guy and pushed him onto the sofa. She draped the panties over his face, which he immediately began sniffing like a pet dog. She hoisted her dress and mounted him in one fluid movement, all the while screaming orders to him in Russian, and poor lapdog that he was, he complied, fumbling to open his fly. This was better than that damned fake TV show. She had his erect member in her hand in no time and started stroking it, harder and harder. Other Guy's eyes were glazed, his pistol had fallen somewhere on the chair, but now he had more earthy considerations on his mind than to bother looking for his weapon.

Then Jacqueline's other hand emerged from behind her back, and I saw a flash of steel before she embedded the stiletto into Other Guy's right eyeball. Blood spurted out, but her red dress seemed to absorb it. I was stuck to my seat, unable to move. Was I next? Other Guy let out a squeal like the air going out of a balloon before going limp, only his cock remaining erect, which Jacqueline let go with a smack. She rose and looked straight at me, straightening her dress.

"You look just like your mother, Roy," I said, not knowing what else to say.

"We have to get out of here," he replied matter-of-fact, unzipping and stepping out of his soiled red dress. Falsies peeped over the lowcut bra he was wearing. I was still in shock.

"But…but you just killed a guy. And probably the other fellah too. Aren't you shaken? I'm…I'm petrified."

"You haven't been out much, have you?" He reached for the large handbag he had dropped inside the door when Porno Guy had dragged him into the suite. He was moving artificially fast, I thought. Perhaps slowing down would only bring out the bile in him, as it was in me.

"But this is murder, Roy." What part of this picture was this kid not getting?

He didn't answer me but pulled out two sets of spandex track pants. He threw one to me. "Here, put this on. We are going for a jog."

I was finally able to rise to my feet. "I need my phone first."

"Don't get too 'petrified' when you go in there."

When I stepped into the bedroom, the bed was soaked in blood. Porno Guy had rolled off and fallen on the floor, a stiletto, similar to the one Roy had used on Other Guy, sticking out of his chest. His clothes remained on his body, but his fly was open, and his cock was erect, rivalling the stiletto for attention and competing with Other Guy for the longest endowment. For a moment I wondered how the maid would react when she came in—two stiffs. I burst out in hysterical laughter that lasted nearly a minute until Roy poked his head in with a quizzical look. With superhuman effort I suppressed the shudder that follows nervous release, tip-toed around the corpse, retrieved my phone, and fled back to the living room. Roy was fully transformed into a man in spandex, even the wig he had been wearing was out of sight, so were the falsies—back in the bag, I guessed.

"Go on, change!" he hissed.

"Where are we going? And how?"

"I have a car parked two blocks down. We will exit the hotel through the front doors and start jogging immediately, no one will pay attention as many business travellers are constantly doing that. You will follow me."

"And you are going to drive to the nearest police station."

"No way!"

"Then where? I have to tell the authorities what is happening regarding the PM scandal."

"I just killed two guys, as you rightly observed. Do you think I can go to a police station now?"

I hadn't thought about that in the anxiety to solve my own dilemma.

"Then where can we go?"

"The only place I have felt safe when similar things happened to me."

"You don't mean Guru Swaminanda?"

"Elementary, my dear Watson. Now, let's go." He swiped the bag off the floor and headed for the door. Midway he stopped, reversed direction into the bedroom and returned, bent over Other Guy and retrieved his pistol. "We'll be needing these guns now that the stilettos are...utilized."

"Are you crazy? Do you even know how to fire them?"

"Just ask Google."

This was all getting way beyond me, but I was past caring. Yet, I stopped him before he headed out. A wave of emotion was hovering, threatening to crash and reduce me to tears. "Why are you doing this for me, Roy? When all I did was abandon you?"

"Because you are the only family I have. And even though I want to kick your ass for doing what you did, you are my only living relative, someone I have never had in my entire shitty life. You—strange though it may sound—are a bonus. Now, can we go?" There were tears in his eyes as he turned away. There were tears in my eyes too. I ran after him.

Getting to the car was a cinch. Luckily, we both dried our eyes and composed ourselves as we took the stairs to the ground floor, avoiding the elevator. The receptionist at the front scarcely paid attention to these two joggers with a bag that could have been holding their gym gear, exiting the front doors nonchalantly, limbering up outside in full view, and then commencing a slow jog down the street.

In the car, a rental, I kept up the pressure. "You can drop me off at a police station and head off to Swaminanda if that's where you feel safest. But I need to clear my name. And as soon as possible."

"There you go! I risk my life for you, and all you can think of is your own hide." The contempt in his voice shut me up. He was right.

I remained silent for most of the ride. We were heading back to Ottawa. Past Kingston I asked him whether Swaminanda was still in Ottawa.

"Yes. I phoned him and told him that I would see him tonight. I didn't tell him what I was up to."

"So, he doesn't know about any of this?"

"No, but he knows a lot. About life. Wait until we meet him. Then everything will be clear."

I decided to call Dee, but the call went straight to voicemail. I decided not to leave a message. I would try her later.

I looked nervously over at Roy driving. He was humming under his breath, trying to act normal, I guess. I could not believe that he was my son. That I had brought a cold-blooded killer into the world. But then, the other side of me rationalized that those two goons were no big benefit to mankind. Roy was ridding the planet of miscreants—a sort of Lone Ranger. That image helped smooth the rest of the ride.

Chapter 10

It was late afternoon when we got to Ottawa. Roy dropped off the rental car, and we took a bus to the guru.

Swaminanda met us with calm equanimity, as usual. "You appear to have had a long and tiring journey. Some lassi, perhaps?"

This time, I didn't refuse. The sweet sherbet was soothing, a comfort. Roy asked to use the shower, and I asked for the same for I couldn't remember how long I had gone without one.

"I will get you some fresh clothes," the guru said. "You like Indian clothes—dhoti, hai?"

"Anything." I growled.

"Very soft cotton. Lots of room for what you call the balls and all, eh." The guru winked and went off to rustle up the replenishments.

The guru gave us each a room that had a bathroom in the centre. When I came out of the shower, I saw Roy sitting on the bed crying. I went to him and put my hands around his shoulders. Deep sobs convulsed within him.

"What's wrong?"

"It's not what's wrong but what's right," he said when he finally blew his nose into a tissue and wiped his eyes with another. "I always get this way, when I come to the guru's, the sense of relief from the shitty world outside. You haven't seen my world."

"I saw a video of you. Having sex with a guy in a hood."

Roy recoiled. "Don't tell me you are a member of the sex club too?"

"The secretlifeofalternativesex dot com?"

"You *are* a member!"

"No, but the guy who stole your Twitter handle, bookmarked the sex club site so that the trail wouldn't lead to him, and used it to view his favourite video every time he needed to jerk off, is a member. At least that's what I figured."

"The bastard!"

"Did they pay you well, at least, for all that prostituting you went through?"

"Two hundred and fifty dollars per shoot. It was better than a night of waiting tables. And it only took a couple of takes. Although, that fucker wanted to retake and retake. . .."

"Was he the hooded guy?"

"Yes. You wouldn't want to mess with him. He makes the Russians look like wall flowers."

"What else did he make you do?"

"His deviancy knows no bounds. I was left puking with shit, piss and cum he had daubed over me by the time he finished, and my ass was sore from taking his big cock for so many retakes in a night, and the whip would crack on my back until I passed out. . .do you want to hear more?" Roy got up and went into the bathroom, leaving me clutching at the empty air for words of comfort. His admission had made me feel the pain as if I had been raped like that. Had I? Maybe in dreams, but I couldn't recall it ever happening in real life unless I had blocked out those experiences.

When we re-convened in the dining room after our baths, I looked a bit stupid in the dhoti, but it covered my nakedness. Every time I tried to walk, I had to lift the garment above my knees lest I tripped.

The guru had also laid a table of chapatis, channa masala and chicken korma for us with more lassi to wash things down. "A simple meal. Come, we will eat first and talk later."

I was ravenously hungry. I hadn't eaten since breakfast. So, I tucked into the food with relish and quickly overate. When I licked my fingers and looked down at my empty plate, I felt bloated and out of breath.

"Some gulab jamun?" The guru pushed those sweet, glistening balls in a bowl towards me, but I shook my head.

"I'll have some," Roy said. "They always remind me of happy times here, Guru." He seemed to have miraculously recovered from his crying of not so long ago. Survivors have no time for self-pity or satisfaction; when either emotion takes them by surprise the survivor shrugs it off lest he is weakened by its influence, lets his guard down and succumbs to the next assault from without. I had many of my historical fiction heroes follow this principle, but here I had someone practicing it in real life.

Leaving Roy to demolish the gulabs, I sat back in my chair.

"You have much on your mind, William," the guru said. "Perhaps you will be lighter if you unburden."

I didn't know whether that would be to empty the contents of my stomach by taking a shit or empty my mind by telling him my story. I chose the latter.

I told him everything from the time after I had left him, the last time in this very ashram. I noticed Roy had gone very quiet.

When I got to the part where we had escaped that morning, the guru looked at Roy, and Roy looked down at his empty gulab bowl. "You have descended into another dark hole, Roy—"

"Another one?" I interjected. "You talk as if he has killed people before."

The guru sighed and softened his tone. "Roy is an avenger. He tries to right wrongs. But he does not do that with kindness, he does it in anger."

"Roy?" I was getting a pain in my stomach. The image of the Lone Ranger was changing to Hannibal Lechter.

Roy shrugged. "I did it for a friend once. A guy was harassing him. So, I off'd the guy."

The guru looked at Roy chidingly. "You tend to 'off' people you don't like more often than necessary, Roy."

"Holy shit!" I exclaimed. "My son is now a mass murderer as well?"

"Oh, shut up, Daddy. The people I off'd were the scum of the earth. My type usually gets killed in some dark alley. I just decided to strike back."

"And you haven't got caught? Yet? Serial killers don't last very long in this country, you know."

"The dumb idiots who get caught *don't* last long, Daddy. When you enter my underworld, you will see the predators who walk around scot free wreaking their sadistic pleasure on the innocent. They never get caught. If I turned full-time vigilante, I could be kept busy offing the multitudes of creeps who live just in Ottawa alone."

I shook my head. This was all a bit much. Then I remembered what I had to do. "Guru, I need to get to a police station as soon as possible."

"There you go again, trying to save your own skin," Roy said and rose. "I'm going for some fresh air."

Just then my cell phone rang in the bedroom where I had left it while changing clothes. That would be Dee, and I ran to pick up before she went to voicemail. The call display said "Private Number" which was correct for she had an unlisted number. I depressed the talk button and recoiled when I heard the voice on the other end.

"Smallwood? Hello! Is that you Smallwood. Answer me, will you!"

It was Darlington.

How the heck had he gotten my unlisted number?

I answered him, shouting into the phone, asking him the same question.

"Oh well, we have your girlfriend with us, you see. Your number was in the contact list in her phone. We thought we'd try it as all other attempts to contact you had failed."

"Dee... is with you?"

"Yes, but she is a bit...ah...indisposed, shall we say. She can't speak to you right now."

"Let me talk to her, Darlington. And if you have harmed her—"

"Oh, cut the bullshit, Smallwood. Stop talking tough. You are in no position to dictate to us. Now, listen to me." Darlington's voice had got harder. "We have the wonderful Divine Secrets in our *safe* custody. One word from you to the police, the newspapers, or even to your priest and she pays the price, *capiche?* And it won't be just a fucking from me, which, by the way, I am looking forward to imminently."

I felt the vice around my heart tighten. The big bad Bully Man was staring at me again. Darlington was the embodiment of Bully Man. I couldn't wilt under his pressure. Not now.

Darlington was speaking, snatching me out of my private wrestling match with Bully Man. "Listen Smallwood. Here's all you have to do: stay out of sight. Don't go near any of those people I told you about. For two weeks. Then you can resume your normal life, and Dee will be released. She will be unharmed."

"What if the police arrest me? They have a warrant out for my arrest and cops are crawling all over the country looking for me."

"Then keep your trap shut for two weeks if you are arrested."

"Why two weeks?"

"Figure it out." The line went dead.

I went back into the dining room clutching the phone. Roy and the guru were still there. So, Roy must have felt the air was good enough indoors after I had left.

"They've got her," I said and collapsed on the chair.

"Who?" Roy snapped.

"Dee. My girlfriend."

"Darlington has her?"

"Yes." I told them about my conversation.

"Two whole weeks?" Roy shook his head.

The guru chimed in. "Ah, it is clear to me now. The election will be over in ten days. There will be no more need to run a misinformation campaign after that."

"Guru, you're amazing. I should have twigged this myself." I said. "Is there anything else you can see in this that I don't?"

"Yes, I see much. In fact, I have a pretty good idea where Dee is being held."

I exploded. "What?"

The guru rose and poured more lassi for all of us. "Please stay calm. We must keep our balance. Here, have some lassi, it will help cool you down."

I forced the cold, sweet nectar down and hung on his words.

"You see, my dear William, it's like this. The retreat that you came to, that property is owned by Professor Darlington. I think you will find Dee there."

As his words sunk in, I remembered the conversation at Alberto's, *I bought a place here. Lakeside property. But it's not the same.*

The guru continued. "When Darlington destroyed me in the press, he did not leave it at that, he cancelled my lease for the retreat. I used to rent the place every year for the last five years to run my retreat. Darlington used to come every summer, for free, for that was part of the rental agreement, to pick up chicks, as he said. He was very jealous when he saw me with Dee. His anger knew no bounds when she rejected his advances and took up with you."

"And now she is in his clutches." I said pacing the room madly. "And you really think he has her secreted away at the resort?"

"The place is usually shut down for the winter," the guru said. "It would be a perfect place to hide her. No one comes at this time, except for wild deer and the occasional stray bear."

"Well, we can at least check it out," Roy said. "You've got two whole weeks of sitting on your ass."

"'We?' You've done enough," I said. "You are going back to your day job."

"No way. You don't even know how to fire a pistol. I just got myself a father. I'm not prepared to lose him so soon."

"Gentlemen!" The guru was holding his hand up. "I think we are not going to solve anything tonight. You are exhausted, and so am I. A good night's sleep and we can approach this with fresh heads tomorrow."

Roy leaned forward. "I'd like to meet this Darlington guy. I want to kick his ass."

I frowned. "You haven't met him? Given how close you and the guru have been, and Darlington coming and going at the retreats, and all? I thought you may have crossed paths long ago."

Roy exchanged an uncertain look with the guru. "Can't say I have. I've only come to meet the guru here, and I have stayed away from other visitors to the ashram. Darlington sounds like a nasty piece of work."

"Well, I can show you some pictures from the yoga retreats," the guru said. "In fact, let me show you pictures from the last one we were at, where you were in attendance, Will. Let me show you quickly, and then we must go to bed, okay?"

He went into his room and returned with an album.

"You still stow photos in albums?" I remarked.

"The best way. I learned that in India." He started rifling through the pages of colour photographs. "Ah, here is one of us sitting down to dinner. You remember, the night you burned your manuscript."

"What was that about? I thought you made your living from writing?" Roy asked.

"A long story," I replied. "One day, I'll tell you."

The guru leaned over with the album, holding it open at a group photo. I recalled the candlelit dinner in the beach cabana. Many of us were in shadow in the photograph, but Dee had been caught front and centre in the light. It looked like that had been the purpose of the guru's picture, a keepsake for old time's sake.

"Is that your girlfriend, Dee?" Roy asked.

I nodded proudly, I had to admit. I glanced at the guru, but he remained impassive. He was watching Roy instead.

"She is gorgeous!" Roy said.

"Thanks."

Then the guru turned the page, and the next photo was of me approaching the fire with my pile of papers in hand. I looked like a high priest about to offer a human sacrifice to the gods. Roy gasped. When I looked sideways at him, Roy's eyes were not fixed on me and my soon to be cremated novel, but on the figure standing at the edge of the bonfire, the man with his camera lowered because Dee had threatened to sue his ass off if he put any of those very personal images on social media. The light was strongest on the features of Professor Darlington.

"No!" The word came in a throttled, choking sound from Roy. He reared back from the album as if he had been stung.

"What?" I said, jumping up myself.

The guru snapped the album shut. "You recognize him, eh Roy?"

Roy got up and fled to his room, slamming the door behind him.

"You wanted him to see that photograph, didn't you?" I said, realization dawning.

"It's about time the circle closes. You and he are running away from the same evil." The guru cradled the album under his arm.

"Did you introduce Darlington to Roy initially?"

"Roy met Darlington in one of those after-hours clubs. But when Roy first came to me in his battered condition and described some of the things Darlington had done to him, it resembled some of the things that had happened at our retreats, when the Professor was seducing, nay raping, my clients. I immediately figured out who Roy's assailant was, but I wasn't going to tell him, it would have served no purpose at the time."

"And it's okay to tell him now?"

"You fail to see the great opportunity that is represented in Darlington and which is also bringing you and your son together in a shared purpose?"

He had a point, but I was still not clear about something. "Why didn't you try to stop Darlington's molestations at the retreats? It wouldn't have been good for your business."

"On the contrary they only reinforced the teaching: that we attract our own demons. Those who fell for Darlington's charms did so willingly. Therefore, they never complained. They had to make their journey out at the other end, as it was one of their own making. Besides, even if I had tried, there was no stopping Darlington when he had his claws into someone. Now I must retire to bed. We will all look at this sensibly in the morning."

But I couldn't sleep. How could it be that of the nearly forty million souls in this country, a handful of us were meeting and interacting in circuitous ways with each other over the generations? What the heck were we trying to teach each other? Was this what karma, or coincidence, was all about?

After tossing and turning for an hour, I slunk out of my room to the living room where a solitary TV stood. I needed a distraction. Horrible images of blood, shit, and urine streaking Dee's body while Darlington had his way with her gave me goose pimples and ratcheted my heartbeat to an unhealthy pitch. I had a headache, and my extremities were sweating uncontrollably. I switched the TV on, turning down the volume really low, mindful not to wake the others. I caught the late-night talk show where the upcoming election was the subject. The PM had now slid twenty points in the popularity ranking since the scandal had broken. More tweets and information were being unearthed of other scandals in the party, while party officials were vehemently denying anything to do with it. The PM was out on the campaign trail and was often seen flustered when the questions addressed, not the excellent job he was doing in government, but this juicy scandal with a pipeline. People were vicious, zeroing down to the lowest common denominator, missing the big picture altogether.

"He's going to lose, isn't he?" Roy had come up and was standing behind me. He put his hand on my shoulder, and it was strangely reassuring.

I nodded. "They, whoever they are, must have an army of misinformation agents working in their employ. I was the patsy. By deflecting the blame and focus to me, and by keeping me out of circulation but at large in the public eye, they can now wreak havoc at will because the police are looking for the wrong guy."

"Is that why he used my Twitter handle to bait you?"

"Yes, so he could leave a trail for the police to find, implicating both of us."

Roy shook his head wryly. "I didn't know my bogey man was Darlington."

"He's *our* bogey man now. The man with the hooded mask. I worry for Dee. I feel so impotent sitting here." I rose and switched off the TV. "I'm scared to sleep. I know I am going to have another bad dream. A horrible one."

"We should go after him."

"Don't be ridiculous. You are scared of his shadow."

"That's been my problem, running away from him. I need to turn and face him."

"I ran away from his type too. All my life, him and his ilk. I used to call his type Bully Man. A faceless creature who only epitomises fear to me."

Roy smiled sadly. "If you have a bad dream tonight, call out for me. I'll come and hold your hand."

I gave him a hug. It was nice hugging my son then. It was very comforting.

"Let's not make any decisions now. As the guru said, a good night's sleep will clear our heads. I'm going to practice the sleep meditation the guru taught me. It will make me rest. You should try it too sometime. Good night!" I watched him go to his room.

But there was no peace for me that night. In fact, the meditation Swaminanda had taught me at the retreat the previous summer and which I had never practiced since, preferring instead the pleasures of Dee's flesh to bring sleep, would have been good for me at that moment, it would have clarified my conflicted mission. Instead, that night, I had my long-suppressed dream. A full-blown technicoloured nightmare in stereophonic sound.

He is a tall dark man, not the guy who greeted me in his waistcoat when the social worker dropped me off in that other dream, not the guy at the foot of the stairs who beat me senseless, but a man in another foster home with large dark eyes that reach cavernous depths, a hunch on his back and black hair that falls over his shoulders in curls. He is bare bodied, chunky flesh with tattoos. I have seen this man before in dreams but this time I see more: his fly is open, an engorged cock sticking through.

There is no place to run. I am in a tiny room, and he is blocking the door. And I am small, he towers over me. I know what he is going to do, and I am powerless to stop him. *I was left puking with shit, piss and cum he had daubed over me by the time he finished, and my ass was sore from taking his big cock for so many retakes in a night.* Where have I heard that before? Those aren't my words, they are Roy's, but that is my experience, too. Yes, for the tall, dark man is doing it to me, and the pain is excruciating. Not once, but multiple times.

I struggle for air, wrestling in his grasp as his weight bears down on me.

Then I awoke.

My body was covered in sweat. I could see the dim light in the hallway separating Roy's room from mine. I had been having another nightmare. The ashram was quiet and Roy's rhythmic breathing was calming. I rose and went out into the kitchen and got myself a glass of water. It was three a.m. Go back to sleep? There were only goblins in my sleep tonight. Better to stay awake. I got back into bed and stared at the ceiling.

Now I am crossing the hallway to another room. There is a cot and a dim light illuminating the baby's crib. I reach inside and pick up the child. The little runt. Doesn't know what will happen to it once it grows up, does it? All those goblins will be a part of his existence too. Better to cash out now after having tasted the elixir of life, mother's milk and human kindness. The rest that follows is not good. Not good, little fellow. Let's walk over to the balcony and a little tip and you will be spared all these ignominies.

I am on the balcony. It's a cool afternoon. The little bundle is raised above my head about to be dispatched into the afterlife when there is a sound behind me. Jacqueline is standing in the doorway I have just exited. She is still in her night dress; her swollen breasts, oozing with milk, press against the flimsy garment, sending a wave of suppressed desire through me. This bundle of joy in my hands has kept me away from those breasts, taken them over. My bundle of misery, would be more apt.

She screams and alarms me. I hesitate, and she is over in a flash, grabbing the baby from me and rushing indoors. I reach out impotently, but she is gone. When I step back into the apartment, I hear the slam of a door and the turn of the key to our bedroom. Not only have I lost those breasts, I have lost their owner. Forever.

Someone was shaking me, and I was gasping for air. "Will, Will... Daddy!"

I shook myself awake. I must have fallen asleep again after getting my drink of water in the kitchen. Roy was at my side.

"You were screaming in your sleep," he said.

"Bloody dreams don't leave me alone," I said, rubbing my eyes, willing myself to stay awake and not roll back into any more nightmares. What the hell had I been reliving just now? But the implications of this last dream fragment had provided the answers long eluding me.

"I know why I gave you up for adoption now," I said. "It was safer."

"What? What's come over you?"

"We'll go together tomorrow...today...after Darlington."

"Are you sure you want to do this?"

"This is our karma. We have to."

"The guru knew all along," Roy said. "He knew the time was right to break it to me tonight. 'When the student is ready, the lesson arrives,' he always told me. Today he introduced the lesson to both of us."

"These lessons are tough ones. Do you think Darlington came into our lives at the right time?"

"The guru says that the lessons don't have to be easy all the time, they just have to be appropriate."

"I'll google how to fire those pistols," I said.

Chapter 11

The guru lent us his car to make the drive over to the resort. "I will wait for you here. This is your meeting with destiny. Your personal meeting. There cannot be outsiders like me present. And yet, if you have not returned by midnight, I will be calling the police," he said.

In the car, I looked up the pistol model on Google. Both handguns were of the same make and vintage: MP-443 Grachs, 2010 model. These were standard Russian military sidearms. They fired eighteen rounds to a clip. I slipped the clips out and checked them; both guns had full clips.

"Point and shoot, I guess," I said turning them over in my hands as Roy drove out of Ottawa heading southwest towards cottage country.

"And make sure the safety catch is off."

"Ah yes. That too." I made sure the safety catches were *on* for now. I didn't want any nasty accidents while we were in this car. In fact, there were safety catches on both sides of these guns for additional security and ease of use.

It was late March and the ice was breaking up in the rivers, but some larger water bodies still had solid ice in the middle.

We stopped at a Tim Horton's for lunch. I had been trying to put the pieces of my dream from last night together, and there were questions that still bothered me.

"You mentioned 'offing' a guy," I opened, concentrating on my BLT. "Didn't it bother you the first time you did it?"

"It was easier when I visualized him as one of the people who abused me as a child," Roy replied, stirring his French onion soup.

Perhaps I was justified in trying to throw him off the balcony as a child. I would have spared him the abuse he suffered growing up. My sleep-deprived condition at the time may have blurred moral boundary lines and suppressed recollection. But why had Jacqueline thrown herself off the balcony instead and left her baby with me, the man who had been trying to destroy the child? Had I off'd her instead in an attempt to get at the child a second time? Had I blocked off that memory too, of killing Jacqueline? Was that going to come out next in another dream, now that I had opened the hatch and let these memories escape? Was I not only a would-be child murderer but a confirmed wife murderer too?

"What was your dream about last night?" Roy asked, looking at me, while I looked outside the window at a group of seniors exiting the restaurant and boarding a coach that was taking them around the country to visit tourist spots—what an innocent pastime compared to what we were embarked on.

"Nightmares about my abused childhood," I said, hoping he wouldn't press me further.

"But you said you understood why you gave me up for adoption. That didn't make my life any easier than yours."

"Life with a screwed-up father wouldn't have been better, trust me. I had a few of those."

He reached out and took my hand. He looked more feminine now. How could this boy-girl go out and kill people? "But I'm glad I found you."

"If Darlington hadn't been using your Twitter handle to spook me, we wouldn't have met. At least we have to thank him for that."

"I think our meeting in the Hog's Head washroom was propitious too."

"That too."

"What happens if we draw a blank at the resort?"

"Then I am turning myself in. This has gone beyond me. I am out of my depth."

Roy took both our trays to empty them in the trash. "Best be going. We have to be back by the guru's midnight curfew."

In the car, my mind went back to that suicide note Jacqueline had written twenty years ago. Some clue to the answers I was looking for, in light of my dream from last night, had to be in that damning epitaph written on the back of the telephone bill. I had read it so many times after the tragedy that each sentence was emblazoned in my mind, never to be forgotten.

Dear Will and Peggy,

I have to call it quits. I don't know reality from acting any more, one blurs into the other. I can't make out the lies I tell people to hurt them from the lies I tell myself in order to get through the day. They say this act of lying makes us good actors or writers, but since I am neither, I am cursed. Please look after Roy. I am sure, between the two of you, you will do a better job than I can. Will, you and I cannot raise this child—we are not good together. Don't hold yourselves responsible for what happened to me. This was of my doing.

Jacquie.

She had addressed the letter to me *and* Peggy. That was it! By binding us both into Roy's future she was protecting him from me. She was consigning him to *both* of us. Peggy was the insurance against madcap me. And yet she never once mentioned my misbehaviour with the kid, my wanting to hurl him off the balcony. *This was of my doing.* She took the fall, cleared the decks for me. She finally took the blame for constantly throwing doubt on Roy's paternity with me. And she was removing herself from any more emotional outbursts that would drive me onto the balcony with the kid again. So, I hadn't killed her after all, but I had led her to see what a danger she was to herself and to us.

Yet, I was the one to blame. As long as I had shown stability, Jacqueline had leaned on me. I had kept at least one of her feet in the sane world. But when I went all maniacal with that kid on the balcony, her fragile world fell apart, there was no stability anywhere anymore for her.

173

That had to be what happened. *Will, you and I cannot raise this child—we are not good together.*

When I began shuddering in the car, I realized that it was stemming from the giant sobs that were wracking me. I couldn't control it, hot tears were pouring out of me, one wave leading to another.

Roy looked across at me, alarmed, and wanted to pull off the road.

I shook my head and blew my nose. "Keep going," I ordered, sounding muffled through the pile of tissues in my hand. "This has been coming for a long time."

"Are you sure? You look like a ghost."

"I just saw one."

"Who?"

"Your mother. She told me she loved me."

"Ah, that's sweet," Roy's voice softened. "Did she say anything about me?"

"Her love for you was never in question."

"Then she wouldn't have thrown herself off a balcony and left me alone."

"She left you with me. And Peggy. But I abandoned you. I am sorry."

Roy reached his free hand across and took mine. I let him hold me until my tears dried up. We were turning off the highway onto a dirt road that ran up to the resort.

I straightened up in the seat and wiped my eyes. "Okay, the time for tears is over. Now we have a dragon to slay."

We pulled into the parking lot of the resort. It would be a ten-minute minute walk from there to the cabins and the main lodge. A navy blue Cadillac was parked beside a grey Ford Explorer SUV in the deserted lot. I recognized the SUV immediately. It was Darlington's. We pulled up behind the Cadillac leaving space in between for the other car should it back up. I could see someone in the driver's seat of the Cadillac, but the Ford was empty.

Roy was gripping his pistol. I hauled mine out too.

"Step out of the car and draw the driver's attention," Roy said. "I have you covered from inside."

I did as he ordered. My knees were shaking when I stepped outside. The driver seemed to be having a conversation on his mobile phone.

I trained my gun on the Cadillac. This little pistol suddenly weighed a ton, and I had to rest my hand on the roof of the car.

"Step out of the car," I yelled to the driver of the Cadillac. So far, I could only see his back, so I didn't know who this guy was. But I was pretty sure he was watching us in the rear-view mirror.

Suddenly the door burst open and the man inside the car jumped, or rather, rolled outside, onto the icy asphalt, somersaulted and came up straight, pointing a gun at me and firing in one fluid movement. I returned the fire, but my gun only clicked uselessly. I ducked under the side of the car as bullets flew on either side of me. My legs had turned to jelly. I stared at my gun quizzically while I heard Roy opening fire from inside the car. Shit! I had left the safety catch on. I flicked the safety off, summoned all my strength, and raised my head over the car roof to return fire. There was no need. A big man lay prone on the ground before us. My attacker looked like he had been potted conclusively by Roy. The smell of cordite was thick in the air.

I limped around the car and advanced on the fallen man as Roy opened the door behind me and followed. The man had fallen face upward and it was easy to recognize the artificially sun-tanned face of Igor.

"This connects Darlington to the Russians. This man was the boss of my captors in Whitby. And that's Darlington's SUV over there."

Roy was looking all around him. He paid scarce attention to the man he had just killed. "Then Darlington could be anywhere near here. We'd better split up. You go on ahead to the resort. I'll bring up the rear."

"Okay. It's straight through that path and downhill to the water."

"He probably heard the shooting and will be waiting for us. Armed, no doubt. Did you take the safety catch off this time?"

I grinned sheepishly. "Yes, it's off this time. And it stays off as long as we are on this property."

As I scampered down the path to the main lodge, the gathering dusk and the colder weather gave this place a much gloomier dampness than when I had come here during Indian Summer last year. The familiar grounds brought thoughts of Dee. I passed the spot where she had first waved to me as she had been putting away her paints for the day. She had been lurking like a faithful parrot on my shoulder these last few days but had been prevented from intruding into my thoughts. And there had been plenty to occupy my head, what with suppressed dreams, Jacqueline's ghost, the various incarnations of Bully Man, not forgetting Russian hoodlums, Roy, and even the guru with his cryptic revelations of the circular nature of things. Whatever bad events that had gone upstream in my life were returning downstream in a tidal wave to drown me. Dee didn't stand much of chance for my airtime with these forces stacked up against her.

Thoughts of Dee now took hold of me and made me sweat despite the cold. I was faced with the stark reality that she was in danger in one of those cabins slowly emerging through the trees. And now I understood how Roy must have felt when he "off'd" those undesirables. I wanted to kill Darlington with a ferocity that didn't faze me.

When I entered the clearing, opposite the middle administrative shack, there was no sight of anyone. All the buildings were in darkness. No, that wasn't true—a dim light peeped out of Cottage #4, Darlington's cabin when I was here last.

I darted across the open yard to the darkened administrative cabin and then hopped across from cabin to cabin until I arrived at #4. I crept towards the window. The shutter had been drawn aside so I could look inside. I raised my head over the windowsill and nearly fell on my butt from what I saw.

The room was dimly lit by a small lamp on a bedside table. The only other pieces of furniture were a large four poster queen bed and a mirror immediately behind it. Dee lay sprawled on the bed. She was clothed only in an oversized white tee shirt—torn and dirty—that reached down to her thighs. She wasn't wearing underwear for I got a clear view of her lushly hirsute crotch; her legs and her arms were spread-eagled and tied to the four corners of the four-poster. There was a gag around her mouth. Why was it that even in this moment of stress, I felt the stirring of desire? There was no one else around. Concern overruled lust and seeing her in such a helpless condition made me toss caution aside. I went around to the front door and kicked it open. It swung open and hit whatever was behind but stayed open. There was no one inside but Dee. Stashing the pistol in my pocket to free my hands, I rushed into the room and made for the bed to untie her hands that looked swollen and bloodless. The look of horror in her eyes made me realize that this had perhaps been an unwise move, for the door swung back behind me and slammed shut.

"Welcome, Smallwood."

I swung around. Darlington had been standing behind the door. He was pointing a gun at me. I noted that it was similar to mine, standard Russian military issue, an MP-443 Grachs—it's weird what the mind registers under moments of stress when it's not lusting after one's half-naked lover. Given that he had the drop on me, it was futile to draw my gun.

"The game's up, Darlington," I bluffed. "I've notified the police."

"Then I'll have to carry out my part of the bargain, won't I?" He didn't look like the slightly eccentric, grey-haired and goateed professor. He had shaved off his goatee and dyed his hair jet black. He looked younger and more purposeful. More dangerous.

Something told me that if I kept him talking with his back to the door, Roy would get here. Roy, who had been my saviour this far would get the better of Darlington. As for me, I think I needed to stick to writing. I was pathetic in action.

"Igor is dead in the parking lot," I said. Would this get his attention?

Darlington didn't flinch. "Yes, the parking lot camera goes on the blink from time to time. I missed that shootout. Those Russians were an inefficient bunch, anyway." He pulled out his smart phone. "But you are lying, the police are not here. I have this property wired with security cameras which I can monitor on this phone...other than for the parking lot. No one entered the front gate but you. I phoned Igor to warn him, but he chose not to take my advice."

"Do you think you can get away with this? The guru is calling the police as we speak."

"Don't make me laugh, Smallwood. The guru lives in his own little world." He glanced down at his phone. "In fact, your accomplice is heading this way right now. I want you to watch what I do to him, and afterwards I want you to watch what I do to your girlfriend here."

Then he casually pointed his gun at my leg and shot me. I felt my left leg explode and collapse. I looked down at my knee, and there was a gaping hole in it with smoke curling out. I crumpled involuntarily onto the floor. I saw the bed leap up and down as Dee struggled with renewed energy to free herself, muffled grunts emanating from her. The shock of being shot lasted for well over a minute before the pain started to spread inside me. I squirmed on the floor, pulling myself towards the wall so I could lean against it and sit up. Through a haze of pain, I saw Darlington studying his phone again. Suddenly he swung around, wrenched the door open, went down on one knee and fired, all in one fluid movement, just like Igor had done. Perhaps they had trained together. But Darlington was successful. I heard a scream outside, followed by a thud.

Darlington casually shut the door again but continued to look at his cell phone. "Yes, I think he is dead, Smallwood. He's not moving."

He's killed my son. My saviour was dead. The realization dawned on me stronger than the pain creeping up my knee. I screamed, not sure whether it was in pain or for the loss of Roy. For both, I think.

"Pains, doesn't it?" Darlington rested the phone against the lamp beside the bed, and laid his gun beside it, both within his reach. "He was a special kid. He called himself Abandoned. Spunky. But he had a troubled history. You were a big part of that."

"How did you know we were related?"

"Oh, I was curious about Abandoned. I was mildly obsessed with him, as a matter of fact, after our sexual encounters. I went digging. His papers said his biological parents were unknown, but I had government connections who could dig a bit deeper. The search led to you, the perfect fall-guy for what was to become Operation Maple Leaf."

"They'll get you, Darlington. The cops will." What the hell was I saying? There were no cops, and he knew it.

"Oh, don't get melodramatic, Smallwood. I've sold this property, you see. The new owner will not need to know anything about you guys. Tomorrow, you will all be dead. I'll just throw your bodies down the disused well and close it up. I was supposed to do that and clean up this place as a condition of sale before I vacated, anyway. I'll be thinking of you on my island in the sun."

"It's blood money you'll be living on, Darlington. Russian blood money. I'll fucking haunt you, like your type has haunted me all my life."

"It's not about Russia or any one country, Smallwood. In fact, national boundaries are the limiting factor in our thinking. We may have perfected this concept of election hijacking with the Russians down in the States a few years ago, but now we are international, and we've done more than a few national elections. My bosses are from all over: Canada, the USA, Monaco, Dubai, Switzerland—anywhere that money can move seamlessly with no questions asked. It's the new world order, Smallwood. You guys call it the 'One Percent,' I call it my tribe."

His excitement was growing as he expounded his philosophy. His eyes were glazed, and his voice had ramped a notch higher. Or it was my imagination, for the pain in my leg was making me lose the thread of what I was trying to say. I felt like I was blacking in and out of reality.

Then he unzipped his pants jolting me awake again. "You know this beats foreplay in all the kinky places I've been in."

"You fucking bastard," I screamed through barred lips. But I couldn't move. I was wading in a sticky sludge and my injured leg was totally dead now.

I saw his cock leap out as he released it from his underpants. This cock was real, and I wasn't imagining anything. I had to hand it to the man, he had a magnificent cock, hard and erect, despite his years. Then he went out of my sightline as he bent over the rocking bed.

"First, I'll give it to her from the front, Smallwood. A pleasure I have anticipated for so long. Then I'll turn her over. Oh, I can't wait. And you, my dear Smallwood, you will watch and hear. It will be most exhilarating."

No wonder Roy had been scared of this man, this monster. He didn't give his opponent a chance. He took his pleasure and his revenge without pause. He was the quintessential Bully Man, my nightmare torturers coalesced into this one being who was now moving over to the rocking bed to defile Dee.

Then the door creaked open, and my heart leapt. Standing there was Roy, his chest a large splash of red. He stood weakly, focusing like a drunk, trying to raise the gun at his side.

Darlington stood up again, interrupted and annoyed. This was theatre of the absurd at its most ridiculous: Roy staggering by the door trying to raise a gun weighing down like a dumb bell too heavy for its lifter, Darlington staring him down in hubristic nakedness, with his erect cock as his only weapon—he hadn't even bothered to pick up his gun from the bedside table—the bed continuing to rock from Dee's ever-weakening gyrations, and me huddled on the floor drowning in my gory effulgence.

"Well hello, Abandoned," Darlington said. "What's with the man's clothing, eh? Didn't recognize you out there. Want to join in the fun? Boy, this is getting way too kinky, even for me."

Roy was muttering something, but only bloody spittle drooled down his chin. I thought I heard "kill, kill you" coming from him.

Darlington chuckled. "Kill me, Abandoned? I heard you had bumped off those idiotic Russians. Good on you! But me? I am your master, Abandoned. You obey me, remember? Now, quit the playacting, step up here, drop your pants and let me give it to you. You like that don't you? You always did. Smallwood, you have a kinky relative in this kid."

To my horror, I saw Roy nodding and meekly stepping forward. He seemed to be under the hypnotic spell of his Bully Man, the man he feared the most who was taking control of his mind in its weakened state.

"Don't!" I yelled.

Roy stopped, rolling his eyes, my words registering somewhere.

"Come!" The Bully Man was calling again. Roy continued his staggering advance towards the bed.

Mercifully, before I could counter, nature got in the way, and Roy collapsed, falling at the foot of the bed, lying still this time.

"Roy!" I screamed.

"Roy? Oh yes, I forgot you call him by that name," Darlington said, looking at me. "He goes by a host of names doesn't he, the little faggot. Ah well, a threesome with a sprinkle of gore would have been fun."

"You killed him!"

"What did you expect?"

Darlington dismissed Roy and me with a shrug and returned to the rocking bed.

Gritting my teeth against the pain, I slithered over and grabbed the bed leg to pull myself up and try, in whatever way, to prevent his act of debauchery. My movement made something hard grate against my thigh. My pistol. It was still in my pocket. Of course! Darlington hadn't seen my gun as I had pocketed it before charging into the cabin to rescue Dee. And he hadn't seen me brandishing it in the parking lot. I had one more chance. *Don't fuck it up this time. And remember to unlock both safety catches, you moron!*

I had the pistol out under the cover of the bed. I flipped the second catch—the first one had already been switched—grabbed the bed leg and pulled my weight up to get my head above the level of the bedspread, just as Darlington's cock was about to enter between my Dee's legs that he was holding widely spread against her struggling resistance and muffled grunts. I caught one look of his manic glee in the mirror above the bed, a look to remember for the rest of my life, before pulling the trigger. The explosion knocked me on my back. I heard a crash on the other side of the bed. Darlington had fallen on the floor, reminding me of a similarly fallen Porno Guy. But he wasn't out like his Russian compatriot. Lying on the floorboards, I could see his supine frame on the other side, struggling to rise. I shot across and under the bed and kept my finger on the trigger, emptying all eighteen rounds into him.

Smoke rose from under the bed, like it had caught on fire. When it cleared, I saw a crimson mess against the far wall. I had finally slain my dragon.

I dropped the gun and pulled myself up back onto the bed and wrenched the spittle-soaked gag from Dee's mouth. I desperately wanted to kiss her, cuddle her, escape from this place.

She was gasping for breath and shuddering, I held onto her to calm her down. Now was not the time for words. It took all my strength to hold her. There we remained, Roy on the floor, me and Dee clutched in each other's arms, with a dead Bully Man adding his blood to the rivers of red already criss-crossing the room—a tableau united in gore.

There was only one thing left to do, a job I had left undone for too long. I reached over to the side table, grabbed Darlington's phone and dialled 911.

Chapter 12

All that happened a year ago.

I guess, like a good novelist, I need to tie up the loose ends before I close this book. And there are a lot of loose ends.

I had some answering to do to the police despite my shattered kneecap. "Why did you empty eighteen rounds into a man at close range?" "Why didn't you call us earlier?" "Why did you evade questioning in Ottawa and flee to Toronto?"

How do you tell them that I needed eighteen rounds to kill a bogey man who had been hounding me for years, depriving me of sleep, making me a failure at everything I did? How do you tell them that this bogey man, this Bully Man, was also the nemesis of my son who was fighting for his life at the moment? And was the cause of the near rape of my partner. Eighteen rounds were generous.

I was not out of the woods yet, but the cops realized that I could be a useful collaborator while they had me in their clutches. After they put my knee in a cast and gave me some painkillers, I spent many hours in the police station, and later with CSIS, unravelling the malicious social media campaign that had been launched to hijack the election. When the news broke three days later, I became an anonymous celebrity that no one could meet as I was under police protection. The fake news outlets went into disrepute overnight and there was a large upswing of support for the prime minister and his party. When Chung, Darlington's IT guy, was roped in for questioning based on a trail of e-mails found on Darlington's computer, I realized how insidious this game had been. Chung was the hacker who was supposed to have been me. However, given how close we were to the election, a week after the story broke, the voting was mixed. The PM managed to hold onto his job but emerged with a minority government. Personally, I liked the outcome; minority governments kept everyone honest, ruling party and opposition alike, and compromise was needed for progress to be made. I was also released from police protection after the election—what could anyone achieve by offing me now? The election results would stand unchanged.

My bigger concern was Roy. He had taken the bullet in his chest, but doctors said he would live. When I visited him in hospital, he asked me whether they could also do a sex change on him at the same time so he could walk away from his earlier life and embrace a new persona free of blemish? I told him that I didn't think it was a good idea given that he was still going to have to answer for the killing of the three Russians and needed to remain as Roy, the cross-dressing male killer, at least on the short term. After he got out of hospital and went through a period of convalescence and rehab, he appeared in court, but a kind judge released him as all three killings were done in self defence. He was, however, ordered to perform three months of community service to atone for taking the law into his own hands and not seeking police help. He is currently one month away from completing that order. He says he wants to train to be a personal support worker when he is finally free. He claims he has had enough pain in his life to be able to help people with theirs. I've offered to fund his training.

As for Dee, her employers in Toronto were sympathetic to what had happened to her: being kidnapped from her hotel and being put through horrible trauma afterwards. They kept her on contract and opened their HQ building without her uncompleted paintings for the training centre. In fact, they had a notice opposite the training centre saying: "to be completed shortly by Divine Secrets." Given her celebrity, or should I say notoriety, there were line-ups for the opening of the HQ building, and many fans awaited the later opening of the training centre with her artwork. Her employers had been literally boxed into retaining her.

I went down on my bended knee (my good one) and asked her to marry me, now that I was free of nemeses. I also asked her whether we could have a baby, as I wanted to prove to her, and to Roy, that I was not going to ditch this one but love it within the womb of our new family. Yesterday, after keeping me in suspense for a whole week, she agreed. "But only if we move into a bungalow. I don't trust you with babies on balconies," she said, kissing me on the lips to drown out any protest.

You might ask me how I planned to support a family and pay for the belated education of my oldest child and buy a bungalow to boot. Well, after my short-circuited but successful attempt at blogging, I re-opened that channel. With my new-found celebrity status, I was quickly sought out for "real-life" stories, and the more fantastic they were, the more people craved them. I could tell them my own stories in bits and bites— at least, the bites I cared to share—or have contributors from around the world send me stuff for publishing as guest posts. I had become a story centre, a sort of James Patterson of weird real-life stories, and no one questioned their veracity. It wasn't quite writing for Netflix, but the ad revenue was earning me more than I had ever earned with my previous books. "What happened," and "What is" were in, with limited prose, lots of pictures and repeating words so that search engines could easily find my content. In fact, a year into this gig now, and I think I have lost all my skills for complex sentences and poetical syntax; therefore, I consigned my historical fiction and the half-baked real-life novel I had begun at the yoga retreat to history. The stories I *didn't* go into were the ones of Roy's "offing" undesirables in his underworld; I didn't know about them, and I didn't ask. They had happened before my time with him. They belong in another book, the one that only he could write.

As for Roy's wish to transition, I think there is more to it than his mere desire to change sex. This transition will take years and many steps, according to what I have read on the subject. And I plan to support him through this process. My hope is that if and when he transitions those stories from his past would also be excised along with his former persona.

So, there it is, everything tied with a ribbon, a happy ending, you could say.

There is, however, one piece that merits its own telling, and that happened two days day after the shootings at the resort, when I was given a ride by the helpful but forceful police to perform a "job" for them, despite my leg being trussed up in a plaster cast, forcing me to walk on crutches.

I got out of the unmarked police car at the ashram in Ottawa, hobbled over on my walking aids, and rang the doorbell.

The door opened, and it took me a while to recognize the man standing there.

"Come in," he said distractedly. I don't think he recognized me with my crutches and all. He had aged ten years in the seven months since I had last seen him. His hair was fully grey, and he had lost about fifty pounds.

I followed him into an anteroom that led to the guru's inner sanctum. He sat and picked up an open magazine that he appeared to have been reading before I knocked on the front door.

"Might be awhile," he said. "I've been waiting half an hour."

"Phil Davis, aren't you?" I said, wondering if he would remember me now. He squinted.

I pressed on. "I was your neighbour at the guru's spiritual retreat last summer."

His eyes lit up briefly. "Oh, yes, the writer. I remember. How are you?"

"A bit banged up, but otherwise okay. The guru warned me about the circular nature of life. So, I guess we were bound to meet again at some point."

"Marge left me soon after that retreat." I was taken aback by this sudden outpouring of information. Too much information, I would have said. He seemed to want to tell the world about the debacle that had befallen him.

I didn't want to let on that I knew. "I'm sorry to hear that."

"She didn't give me any warning. Took up with our neighbour who also left his wife." There was more sadness than bitterness in his voice.

"Is the guru able to help?"

"He is the only one who knows both our stories. He is the best person to help. I guess I shouldn't have shown up without an appointment today. But I was going mad inside a lonely house. It was either see him or get drunk again. And my doctor has warned me against the alcohol. That's why I've been waiting here."

I looked at the clock. It looked like it would be a long wait before I got to see the guru. I hoped my police escort would be patient and wait. I had deliberately not taken my pain medication this morning and the numbing effect was starting to wear off from last night's dose. But I needed to stay sharp for my encounter with the guru.

Just then the door to the inner sanctum opened, and, to both Phil's and my surprise, out walked Marge Davis. Her eyes were red, and she seemed to have put on all the weight that Phil had lost. On seeing Phil, her features brightened. He too got up from his chair and looked expectantly at her.

"Phil?"

"Marge?"

It was obvious as mud that this couple had a bond between them that was hard to break, separations and elopements with randy neighbours notwithstanding.

The guru emerged. His guard dropped momentarily when he saw me, a look of surprise or dismay, it was hard to tell. Then his impassivity returned, and he smiled at Phil.

"Ah Phil, you re-affirm my belief that when the pupil is ready the lesson arrives. Your...unscheduled...arrival today is propitious. Marge has seen the error of her recent actions."

"Oh Phil, Maurice was such a horrible...fraud." Marge burst into another flood of tears.

Phil rushed up to her, took her hands and offered soft words. "It's okay, baby. It's okay."

She sniffed, rubbed her damp eyes on his shirt sleeve—perhaps, it was a habit she had indulged in frequently in the past, had missed, and was now resuming quite unconsciously, even hungrily—then looked up at him and frowned. "Oh Phil, you haven't been taking care of yourself. Have you been eating properly?"

The guru spoke commandingly, "Phil, you *don't* need to see me today. You need to spend time with your wife. I suggest you both remove yourselves to a nearby restaurant and have a quiet meal, a long one. And remember, no recriminations. All that has happened is in the past. A new cycle begins for you."

Phil and Marge left holding each other's hands, transfixed on each other's faces. Marge, like her husband before her, hadn't recognized me, for she had eyes only for her emaciated but happy Phil. I didn't say anything to upset their newfound equilibrium; they had plenty of lost ground to recover at that moment. I felt a tinge of happiness for them.

When they had exited the front door, the guru sighed. "You have been in the wars, I see. I guess you need to see me. I read the newspaper this morning. It had good coverage of the shootings at the yoga retreat."

He led me into his sanctum, where the smell of incense was strong. The incense helped, for the pain in my leg had been increasing throughout the morning.

He seated himself on a cushion on the floor and beckoned me with his hand to sit opposite him.

I shook my head. "These crutches don't allow me much flexibility. And I'll make it quick, for I am in pain. I came only to ask one question: why?"

"There are many 'why's' in this story, Will. Which 'why' in particular?"

"I get why you sent us to meet Darlington. You wanted us dead, of course. But why did you throw your lot in with his gang in the first place? You, who preach of leading an integrated and ethical life?"

The guru sighed and settled back on his cushions, leaning into the wall. "I didn't want you dead, Will—that is for the universe to decide—who lives and who dies, and when. I wanted you to be resolved. I am not interested in earthly governance structures. Political parties are just that, different permutations of the same power game. Your Prime Minister, or Darlington's One Percent. Take your pick. I am more interested in the evolution of the soul. You and Roy had reached the pinnacle of integration between yourselves when I sent you forth, in my vehicle, to the resort. It was time for you to meet your nemesis and wrest him or be consumed by him. It was time for the next lesson, for all of you, Darlington included."

"Yet, you were also the person who had bought Darlington's lakefront property. I checked the land title records before I came out today with a little help from the authorities. His antics of discrediting you in the newspaper was all a sham, a subterfuge to show discord between the two of you while all the while you were working towards recruiting me."

"Yes, we played through a script that we had architected to get you onto his team, after Darlington discovered your disguised paternity. It was touch and go whether you would respond to our e-mail solicitation to come out to the retreat, but it worked. You were at that low point then, looking for the next chapter in your life."

"And if I hadn't responded to your e-mail?"

"Oh, Darlington would have found another way. You were a juicy candidate, and he wouldn't have let you go easily. Beneath his professorial quirkiness, he was a predator stalking his prey."

"How many others did you recruit?"

"Many. The information campaign—or *misinformation* campaign, based on one's perspective—had more bloggers than you could think of. You were the only one recruited at the retreat. We recruited others right here. All were troubled souls looking for purpose, like you."

"You even set me up with Dee."

"I didn't. And that was not part of the plan. She *chose* you over me at the retreat. That was a good and clear choice on her part, even though it was hard for me to accept and let go. And that was added fuel to Darlington choosing you as the scapegoat for his scheme. Dee threw Darlington off his game. He was angry for being jilted—another lesson he had to learn. Anger corrodes, as you know. Your anger towards having been orphaned kept you trapped in a spiral of bad dreams. But I regret setting Darlington up with Roy initially. And for misleading you the last time we met. I told you that I had some things to improve on in this lifetime—these were some of them."

"You weren't going to call the police if we didn't make it back by midnight, were you?"

The guru remained silent on this question, the silence indicating either a "yes" or a "no." I would never find out.

I tried another tack. "I thought Roy met Darlington independently of you?"

This time he spoke, ponderously, with his eyes half-closed. "No. I was the one who made the introduction, unbeknownst to Roy. I was trying to move Darlington through and out of his dark ways. His has been a very complex soul to guide from the time I met him five years ago. Sometimes, the only way to address his type of defects is to force him to face them, go through them, and emerge on the other side. I supplied him with women at the retreat as part of that remediation, then I supplied him with men. I believe he not only had sex with them, but he made movies of his exploits as well. All the while, I was waiting for him to emerge from his tunnel, but he liked the danger of mixing his dark side with his official side, making sure they didn't collide, like a gambler playing Russian Roulette. Roy, who came to the ashram seeking help, became one of the 'actors' in the movies Darlington made, after I introduced them to each other, or after I set Darlington upon Roy. You see, during the many confessions that Roy had with me it was easy to get the names and locations of the 'clubs' he frequented. I passed that information onto our esteemed professor. But I miscalculated; Darlington liked to consume his sin, engorge himself on it and hunger for more; he would never renounce it. Roy was not ready for Darlington the first time, and I miscalculated there. But you were *both* ready the next time, when I sent you and Roy to the resort in my car. I knew the situation would resolve itself one way or the other, and the next cycle would begin for all of you. And it did."

"What was in it for you?"

"Darlington promised to hand over the retreat to me if I helped him with this project by recruiting technically competent people with...ah...vulnerabilities. People like you. Many of the people on his government project team." The guru paused, a half smile on his face as he recalled the names of his 'recruits.'

"Was a fat guy called Chung one of your recruits?" I asked.

The guru beamed. "Yes. I remember Chung, a thoroughly one-track specimen—all brain and no heart. There were others too. This property was Darlington's payment to me for those services rendered. He was going to earn a lot of money from this project, he told me, far more than the value of the yoga retreat property, and that would buy him his island in the sun. He could leave this cold country to less fortunate ones like me. So, he signed over the deeds of the resort property to me last week in keeping with that promise. I paid him one dollar for the transaction to keep it legal—I suppose this is no secret if you have been looking up the transaction. He fulfilled his part of the deal, and I did mine. As I have no money, the opportunity to practice my calling in a freehold property like that, to help people, people like Phil and Marge, even Roy and yourself, was reward enough to do what I had to."

"But you were aiding a murderer. Darlington was a murderer. He may have even killed his wife."

"He *killed* his wife. She had no quality of life left when I first met her, trapped in a bed taking insulin shots, unable to attend to her personal hygiene. Unable to lead the contemplative life anymore. A double dose of insulin was all that was required. I saw it as a mercy killing, like putting a sick dog to sleep—you people do that with your pets, don't you? And you don't bat an eyelid over it. Mrs. Darlington was better off moving onto her next incarnation."

"Come on, Guru. There is more to it than that. You knew you were sending Roy and me to our deaths. Darlington was not going to take my voluntary efforts at lying low until after the election at face value, even though he had threatened me with Dee's life. He wanted to personally put me out of action. He wanted me dead. You knew this and conspired to help him."

"If that makes you understand what happened, then feel free to believe that version of events."

I was losing my patience with his blithe justifying of his actions. "I don't get it, man! All this mayhem that we have gone through—which could have been avoided if you'd come clean in the first place—is because you claim that your aim in life is to provide people with lessons for their souls while you ignore the fallout on the earthly plane that comes with these...lessons."

"As I said, I don't subscribe to mortal concerns. They are but passing events in a series of lives we all pass through in order to reach the perfect state."

"Well, I am going to give you a taste of betrayal, Swaminanda. Inside this big plaster get-up is a microphone, and I have been relaying this conversation word for word to the police vehicle that brought me over here and is parked not far from your front gate. By signalling to it now, I will ask that its occupants waste no more time, enter your premises, and arrest you."

The guru's face fell at the mention of the microphone. Then his impassivity returned. "As you wish, but I do not believe I have committed any serious crime."

"Huh! Recruiting candidates to spread spurious news about political leaders, luring Roy and me to our sure deaths at the retreat, pimping for Darlington by providing him victims for his sexual deviancy, and possibly helping him murder his wife—I think there is a lot here that you will be answerable for."

"This earthly system has strange laws. I would say in my defence that I was employed in the business of facilitating spiritual evolution. But who am I to argue with mortal moral constructs? On second thought, it can't be all that bad, this jail thing, can it? I hope there will be a place for me to meditate while in prison, if they send me there. I think I may be able to save many souls in prison, more than on the outside. Maybe that is the next lesson for me in my life's path."

The police entered at that point and took him away. He left with the same equanimity and moral superiority I had always seen in him. Darlington and the guru had made strange bedfellows in crime; bonded only by the prospect of gain, but each with his own interpretation of what that gain meant. Perhaps the guru was indeed an evolved soul despite his self-admitted shortcomings, and we were the ones running around over inconsequential matters. Who was I to argue about mortal moral constructs, as the guru had so rightly pointed out?

I lay my crutches aside and collapsed onto the cushions, fished out my bottle of prescription opioid and took a double dose, compensating for the one I had missed earlier this morning. I hoped it wouldn't kill me like the overdose that took Mrs. Darlington—I had much to live for now. I phoned Dee and told her where I was, said that I loved her, and promised I would be back at my apartment in Ottawa by the following morning. I would leave Roy for tomorrow, when I would have to come up with a way to break the news to him, that this safe haven of the ashram and his guru had ended up being just another illusion; hopefully his "re-instated" Daddy and Dee, and the babies we were planning to make together, would be a compensating new family for him.

There had been a lot of lies and concealed truths bandied about in this story: Darlington, Swaminanda, Roy, Dee, Jacqueline, minor players like Chung, even me—oh yes, my writer's imagination may have coloured some of the events I described, or my abused childhood may have, but we all see the world through different lenses. Yes, we had all lied in our own ways to achieve what we were now left with: a bitter-sweet irony. I hoped there was a drug to wipe those memories out. I hoped the opioid would help.

Then I settled back into the soft cushions in this empty ashram for the best dreamless sleep I was to have in months.

—*End*—

Author's Note

I wrote this novel during a period of convalescence from a sudden cardiac arrest that overcame me on September 11th 2018 – my 9/11. Writing the novel helped in my recovery, for I was able to reclaim some artistic freedom during a time when writers were losing out to a groundswell of political correctness. We were being squeezed into foxholes where the only permissible character we could write about without sanction was ourselves.

Therefore, this book spans a range of character, race, gender, political, social, and philosophical spectra without inhibition, helped no doubt by a bagful of pharmaceutical drugs and the loss of self-censoring filters—a writer's Nirvana. I also advanced dates of certain events, like the 2019 Canadian Federal Government Election, from the Fall to the Spring to provide for fictive flow. Everything else came from my imagination.

I wish to thank the anonymous firefighters, paramedics, doctors and nurses who saved my life during the writing of this book. If you hadn't given me a second chance at life, I wouldn't have completed this novel about second chances.

I also wish to thank my advance readers of this manuscript and my editor Jennifer Bogart for her diligent work and encouraging feedback. This was not an easy book to write, and your support relieved the burden on me.

Shane Joseph—2020

Biography—Shane Joseph

Shane Joseph is a graduate of the Humber School for Writers in Toronto and studied under the mentorship of Giller Prize and Canadian Governor General's Award-winning author David Adams Richards. ***Redemption in Paradise***, his first novel, was published in 2004. ***Fringe Dwellers***, his first collection of short stories, was released in 2008, and is now in its second edition. Shane's second novel, ***After the Flood,*** a dystopian novel of hope, was released in 2009 and won the Write Canada Award for best novel in the futuristic/fantasy category. Shane's 'autobiographical novel,' ***The Ulysses Man***, was published in 2011, and is a fictional chronicle of the

Burghers of Ceylon. Shane's fifth work of fiction, **Paradise Revisited**, a collection of short stories that continues to explore the immigrant experience, was short listed for the Re-Lit award in 2014. He covered his travels in Peru in a novel, **In the Shadow of the Conquistador**, published in 2015. His latest collection of short stories, **Crossing Limbo**, was released in June 2017. His most recent novel was **Milltown**, published in April 2019.

Shane's fiction, non-fiction and book reviews have appeared in literary journals such as the Book Review Literary Trust of India, The Wagon Magazine, Devour, and in anthologies all over the world. His blog at www.shanejoseph.com is widely syndicated and he has a monthly column in The Sri Lankan Anchorman newspaper.

More details on Shane's work, blog and public interviews can be found on his website at www.shanejoseph.com

CPSIA information can be obtained
at www.ICGtesting.com
Printed in the USA
BVHW041403051020
590307BV00015BA/312